P9-DVQ-960

THE VIGILANTE

Ex-lawman Jake Harper had been railroaded by a gang who had murdered a miner and his wife and stolen a fortune in gold. By trickery and buying off the authorities, the outlaws went free and Harper went to prison.

Later pardoned, Harper sets out to track down the killers and make them pay. But a crooked U.S. marshal tries to thwart his pursuit, hoping to see him once more behind bars. To make matters worse, Harper finds himself falling for the daughter of one of his sworn enemies.

Violence and bloodshed erupt in many places before the final showdown . . .

THE VIGILANTE

Ray Hogan

GUNSMOKE

This hardback edition 2003
by BBC Audiobooks Ltd
by arrangement with
Golden West Literary Agency

Copyright © 1975 by Ray Hogan.
Copyright © renewed 1988 by Lily Scott.
All rights reserved.

ISBN 0 7540 8252 0

British Library Cataloguing in Publication Data available.

Printed and bound in Great Britain by
Antony Rowe Ltd., Chippenham, Wiltshire

～ 1 ～

Jake Harper stood quietly in the early-morning sunlight outside the high stockade wall of the prison listening to the sounds of the iron-strapped timber gate swinging shut behind him, the scraping and thud as guards slid the heavy crossbar into place, the jingle of metal as chain and lock were secured. Then, hard-bitten, bearded face set, he started down the long slope for the settlement at the foot of the hill.

He'd spent better than two years inside the prison, years he now wanted to forget but knew well he never could. A man—a lawman, in fact—accustomed to riding free, going where he wished whenever he pleased, the confinement had been pure hell. He'd never gotten over the restlessness, nor accepted the sort of life the towering walls with their catwalk-patrolled guards attempted to impose. Others there had, having lapsed into a dazed, lethargic state of mind—little more than dead men moving about woodenly, listlessly and accepting the abuse visited upon them stoically.

Harper had never permitted himself the luxury of retreating into that refuge of resigned catalepsy, had instead fought stubbornly against it. Grim and silent, he did what was required of him and no more, absorb-

5

ing impassively whatever punishment was meted out when due, resisting when it was not, despite the probability of more severe steps being taken against him for so doing.

Always a solitary man, he became even more a loner while inside Big Lonesome, as the prison was called, holding himself apart from the other inmates, neither asking for nor expecting favor or help from anyone, fighting his own battles—often as not against some prisoner who remembered Jake Harper as the man responsible for his being there.

He'd had no visitors during the two years and seven months he was inside, nor had he received or dispatched any letters. He had simply dropped from the face of the earth when Deputy U.S. Marshal Caleb Lynch, carrying out the sentence decreed by Circuit Judge Amos Chancellor, had delivered him to the warden at Big Lonesome and the gates had swung shut behind him.

There were those he had left, however; the people of Red Rock, where he'd been town marshal for several years and who he'd thought were his friends. And there was the widow of a rancher upon whom he'd occasionally called—a relationship that might possibly have prospered and grown to fuller meaning had not the Josh Moon affair occurred and brought his life to a standstill.

He'd never forget the smiles and snickers of Red Rock's merchants as he rode off in shackles with Lynch that day. They were glad to see him go, perhaps not to the extent of his going to prison, but to be rid of him.

He was a hard-nosed marshal, they felt—and all to their detriment. And perhaps he had been a bit on the overzealous side, but he was a man who believed in the

law, lived by the letter of it, and brooked no devia-
tions. If a man was guilty of a crime, he had to be punished; to him it was that simple, just as it also was his
duty to see that punishment put into effect. An outlaw
was his personal enemy and considered by him to be
nothing more or less than an object to be apprehended
at any cost and brought to justice for an accounting.

It was at that stage of procedure that things had
suddenly gone wrong for Jake Harper. The law had
failed—no, it was the administration of the law that
had fallen short and turned against him. He could not
blame the law for destroying his faith in its fairness
and invincibility, only the man who had sat in judg-
ment and prostituted it. The law in itself was still just
and essential; human failure in high places was its
weakness.

Harper paused midway down the grade. About him
the ground was starkly bare of all rocks and vegeta-
tion, cleared in years past and kept so by convict labor, leaving the hill a bleak, sun-ravaged cone on the
tip of which Big Lonesome perched like some huge,
hump-shouldered vulture.

Narrowing his eyelids to cut down the glare, Jake
studied the settlement just ahead. It had grown little if
any since he had last seen it. The few starved-looking
trees appeared a bit larger, and the brush that had
crowded its edges had retreated farther back on the
flat. If there were any new buildings, he was not aware
of them.

There was no good reason why the settlement,
Higgtown, should flourish. It existed only because of
the forbidding, weathered structure on the crest of a
nearby hill—a saloon, a hotel and livery stable, a general store with a depository of sorts where prisoners
relegated to Big Lonesome for a limited time could

leave whatever valuables they possessed (for a paid-in-advance fee, of course), and a thin scatter of houses inhabited by the families of the prison guards who happened to be married.

It was a depressing place tainted with the same dismal atmosphere that lay over the scoured hill, and only those required by necessity to live within its bounds did so. It was well off the traveled routes, and only infrequently did freight wagons hauling supplies from the capital break the monotony of its dreary existence.

He'd not tarry there long. Harper had determined that days before he was released. It would be for only whatever time it required to reclaim his money, gun, and other gear at the general store and buy a horse. That would be it. He'd pass up the saloon and the women who hung around it, suppress his thirst for liquor and need for female companionship until he reached a place far beyond the shadow cast by Big Lonesome on the hilltop. Only then would he feel that he was free and could breathe.

Moving on, he reached the bottom of the grade. The square, squat shape of the hotel with its adjoining stable, first in the line of structures scattered about in no orderly manner, was before him. A man slouched against the hitch rack fronting it, his lean, bent shape slack, wide brimmed hat tipped forward to shield his eyes from the driving sunlight. There was no one else in sight, and a gloomy hush lay over all.

Anger stirred through Jake Harper as he watched the lone man draw up slowly, turn. It was Caleb Lynch, thinner, older, but with the same narrow, smirking countenance. Brother lawmen once, they had never been friends, and such was not likely to ever change now.

The deputy marshal nodded coldly. "Want a word with you, Harper."

Jake merely slowed his stride. "You've got nothing to say that I want to hear."

The lawman stiffened, anger now flushing his cheeks and brightening his eyes. "Thought maybe all them months inside Big Lonesome might've changed you. Can see it didn't. Still the same bull-headed son-of-a-bitch!"

Harper, reacting instantly, pivoted. His knotted fist came about, drove forward like a piston. His rock-hard knuckles caught the marshal on the point of the chin. Lynch went reeling backward, tripped, and went down flat into the loose dust.

"No change," Harper said laconically, and again wheeling, continued on toward the general store.

2

Simmering with anger, Jake Harper reached the long, narrow store building with its few and seldom-washed windows, paused at the screen door. He did not look back to where Caleb Lynch was pulling himself to his feet, and there was no regret in him for having knocked the older man to the ground. Lynch had asked for it.

Drawing open the sagging framework of wire and leather hinges, Jake stepped inside the dry, musty-smelling building. The change from bright sunlight to deep shadow was abrupt, and he halted again to let his eyes adjust. From somewhere in the gloomy depths of the room a voice, unfriendly in timbre, greeted him.

"Yeh?"

Vision reconciled, Harper moved on toward the rear of the structure, where a squat, balding man in a collarless shirt and worn overalls regarded him from behind a counter.

"Name's Harper. Come for my stuff."

The storekeeper nodded. "Seen you coming down the hill. What's the box number? Got to have the number, else you're out of luck. That's my rule."

Jake shrugged indifferently, glanced about at the

shelves partly filled with aging merchandise. There had been a number, he recalled vaguely, but what it was, he now had no idea.

"Name's Harper. That ought to be enough."

"Nope. Got to have the number."

"Been two and a half years—"

"Ain't my fault—and rules is rules."

"The hell with your rules," Harper snapped, and circling the counter, pushed by the storekeeper to where a number of padlocked boxes were stacked against a wall.

"Now, wait a minute . . ."

Ignoring the man, Jake picked up a claw hammer, pulled the first box from the stack. "Unless you want me busting open every one of these, you better find out which one of these is mine," he said coldly. "Expect you've got a list or a book somewhere that'll tell."

The merchant glared, muttered something under his breath, and turning to a rolltop desk, angrily jerked open a drawer and took out a small paperback ledger. Flattening it out on the dusty counter, he began to run his finger down a list of names.

"Number twenty-three," he said finally, closing the book.

Opening a small tin box, he rummaged about among several tagged keys, located the correct one, and then, crossing to the stack, inserted the key into the proper padlock and removed it from its hasp.

"You know what you got in here?" he asked, passing the container to Harper. "Without no receipt, I—"

"I know," Jake replied brusquely. "Three hundred and forty-seven dollars and my gun and belt."

Setting the box on the counter, Harper reached into it, took out the cartridge belt, loops still filled with shells, pistol yet in the holster. He examined all carefully, almost fondly, for several moments, and then swung the belt about his waist and fastened the buckle. Settling the weapon to his satisfaction on his hip, he then removed the one remaining item in the box, a black leather poke. Pulling slack into the drawstrings, Harper shook out the currency, the gold and silver coins, and counted them.

"All here," he said, restoring the money to the pouch. "Now I'll take what you owe me."

"Owe you!" the storekeeper echoed, frowning.

"Paid you fifty dollars for five years' rent. Only used half that. I've got twenty-five dollars coming."

"No refunds," the merchant said flatly. "Ain't my fault you won't be using the box."

Harper came slowly around, hand dropping to the butt of his pistol. "The trouble you're going to have if I don't get that money back'll be your fault," he said softly.

The storekeeper's mouth tightened. "You're just aching to get sent back up there on top of the hill, ain't you?" he said, and dug into a pocket. Counting out two gold eagles and five silver dollars, he dropped them on the counter. "And I'm betting that's where you'll be again before you even get the stink of the place off'n you."

"Not likely," Harper said, adding the coins to his poke, and wheeling, walked the length of the room and stepped out into the open.

Caleb Lynch, leaning now against the rack that fronted the store, met him with a cold nod. Wary, Harper came to a stop.

"Back there," the lawman said grudgingly, jerking a thumb toward the livery stable. "I reckon I hadn't ought've said what I did. Was out of line."

"It was," Jake answered, resuming stride.

Lynch fell in beside him. "Still some things that've got to be said . . ."

Harper glanced at the federal marshal. There was a discolored area on one side of the man's chin where Jake's fist had landed.

"Can't figure anything you've got to say that I'd be interested in," he said stiffly, moving on into the street.

Life now showed along the dusty way. Two men were standing at the side of the saloon in conversation; a slatternly woman, her gaudy dress dull from use and lack of cleaning, lounged in the entrance to that building while she eyed him invitingly.

"Want to hear what you're aiming to do," Lynch said.

Harper shook his head. "Don't see as that's something you need to know. I've been pardoned, not paroled."

"All the same to me," the lawman said. "You're aiming to track down that bunch, ain't you?"

Harper made no reply as he turned into the wide entrance of the livery stable. Immediately, a man, stripped to the waist and wearing baggy, stained army pants and dung-covered boots, emerged from a small office at the head of the runway.

"You'll be wanting a horse and gear, I take it," he said, nodding. "Seen you coming down the hill a bit ago. . . . Now, I got a nice little buckskin that ought to suit you to a T. A mite boogery, maybe, but he's got plenty of bottom. . . . That's him right there in that first stall."

Jake glanced at the animal, looked away. The horse was too small. "What else've you got?"

The stable owner clawed at his unkempt beard, pointed to the rear of the rank-smelling building.

"Well, there's a couple, three more out there in the corral I might consider selling."

Harper moved on down the runway, gained the enclosure, and opening the gate, stepped inside. There were a half-dozen horses dozing slack-hipped in the shade, none of which appeared particularly good. Glancing over the lot, Jake selected a tall black, moved in close, and made his examination. He took his time, enjoying the chore, as the feel of freedom gradually worked itself into his blood.

"I'll go seventy-five for this gelding," he said finally. "You throw in a saddle, blanket, and bridle."

The stableman swore in shocked disbelief. "Seventy-five dollars! My God, man, that animal's worth twicet that—and with the gear . . ."

"Horse I sold you little more'n a couple of years ago was better than this one, and you only gave me fifty for him."

"Was a long time ago, and thing's 've changed."

"Not that much. What do you say? Either take it or else I'll hang around till the freight wagon comes in and catch a ride back to the capital. Expect I can do better dealing there, anyway."

The stableman brushed at a fly tangled in the hairs on his chest, swore again. "Tell you what—how about you going a hundred and I'll let you pick your own saddle and the rest."

Jake gave that thought. The horse wasn't worth it, but the sooner he got away from Higgtown and the overshadowing walls on the top of the nearby hill, the better he would like it.

"All right. Make me out a bill of sale. I'll do my own saddling."

The man nodded, pointed toward a half-dozen hulls lined up on a cross timber just inside the barn.

"Take whichever one of them you want," he said, starting toward his office. "Bridles and blankets're there, too."

Harper caught up the black's halter, led him into the rear of the barn. Snubbing him loosely to a convenient post, he made his selection of gear.

Lynch, quiet throughout the bargaining session, stepped in nearer. "Asked you a question, Harper."

Jake, spreading the blanket on the gelding's back and smoothing out the wrinkles, swung the saddle into place.

"They still owe the law, far as I'm concerned."

"The law!" Lynch repeated angrily. "That ain't it— you're figuring they owe you for them two and a half years in prison, and you're going to—"

"No, that's not bothering me none. It's the judge I owe for that."

"Then you ain't got no call to go gunning for them."

"They still owe the law," Harper said again. "It's still got a claim on them."

Caleb Lynch's lined face was flushed. "You standing there telling me you're going after them for the killings they done—that it ain't nothing personal?"

"That's the way it is."

The old lawman shook his head slowly. "If you're meaning that for true, then it's wrong. Judge found them not guilty."

"Means nothing to me!" Harper snapped in a harsh voice. "I was there . . . heard what Jim Rooney said before he died. I know they're guilty, same as they know it, and I aim to see they pay up for what they did."

"You ain't got the right, Harper . . . and doing it'll be wrong. They been tried once, and the judge turned them loose. They can't be tried again for it."

"Wore a star myself once—for a plenty of years. I know that, but it means nothing to me. And far as your Judge Amos Chancellor goes—he was wrong. Like as not he was bought off—that bunch took over fifty thousand off that miner after they killed him. They had plenty to dicker with."

"Was Amos Chancellor that went to the governor and got you pardoned. Ain't showing much thanks starting out to do what you've got in mind."

"I never asked him for a pardon—him or nobody else. Expect he was having trouble sleeping nights, and that was what pushed him into doing it."

Lynch sighed raggedly. "Well, you're heading for trouble. Can't appoint yourself a one-man vigilante committee and go chasing after—"

"Can and will," Harper said bluntly, stepping up to the black's head. Removing the halter, he slipped the bit into place, began to buckle down the headstall of the bridle.

"You always was badge-heavy, Harper," Lynch said quietly. "Seemed to think you was the only lawman in the country and you had some special calling to haul in every man you come across that didn't just suit you."

"Was my job. If they were breaking the law, I—"

"The law! Goddamnit, there's more to the law than dragging folks into court!"

"Not if they're breaking it," Jake said, rubbing the nose of the black. "Which don't count for much now, anyway, since I'm not a lawman."

"You best remember that. Never have liked you, Harper. Always figured you was out for my job."

"Never was. Might've taken it once, had it been offered to me, but it's too late now. Got other fish to fry."

"And I'll be watching you do it—just hoping you make a mistake. I was against them pardoning you, but nobody'd listen to me. Don't matter. You'll stub your toe, and I'll trot you back up that hill to Big Lonesome so fast it'll part your hair!"

"Don't lay any bets on it, marshal," Harper said coldly. "Don't figure to make any mistakes. I know the law good as you do, and any move I make'll be within it."

"Vigilante justice—that sure's hell ain't within the law!"

"Not claiming it is, but I'm going to see that justice is done. It never had a chance in Amos Chancellor's court."

"You got what the law figured was right."

"That wasn't justice."

"Maybe to your way of thinking," Lynch said. "You're forgetting a judge runs a court according to the laws he's given to work with—that makes it a court of law, not a court of justice. If you don't figure the law gives out justice, then best thing to do is get the laws changed."

Jake Harper smiled wryly. "You're talking like one of those shyster lawyers, marshal. That judge beat the law, either because he got paid off or because the law got all twisted about in his head and caused him to turn five killers loose. I'm going to change that, make the law mean something again and—"

"Here's your bill of sale," the stableman broke in. "For one black gelding branded JX on the left hip. All I'm needing is your name."

Harper supplied it, waited while the hostler added it to the paper, and then, taking the document from him, examined it closely.

"Appears all right," he said, and thrusting it into a

pocket, counted out the agreed-upon cash. He pointed then to the wall beyond the saddle rack. "Canteen hanging there—it go along in the deal?"

The stable owner shrugged, stuffed the money into his snap purse. "Reckon so," he said, evidently well satisfied and pleased with the transaction he'd made. "I'll fill it up for you, if you like."

Harper nodded, fell to adjusting the length of his stirrups. He paused, glanced toward the grim walls capping the long hill as a gunshot flatted hollowly through the morning hush. An attempted escape, likely, and fated, as were all the others he'd seen desperate men try during his time there, to end in failure—and death.

Caleb Lynch seemed not to notice the rifle's report. "What way'll you be riding?"

Jake uttered a low, derisive sound. "Away from here," he said noncommittally.

"Ain't no point in not telling me. All I got to do is watch . . . and follow."

The saddle now to his satisfaction, Harper swung onto the black. Settling himself, he looked down at the lawman, a hard grin cracking his lips.

"Reckon that's your privilege, marshal," he drawled, "only don't get underfoot."

Cutting the gelding about, Jake rode the length of the stable's runway and out into the bright sunlight. Pausing at the water trough, he took the canteen from the hostler, and nodding his thanks, continued on down the street.

~⁅ 3 ⁆~

Hank Lavendar ... Denver Bannock ... Yancey Richter ... Matt Sandman ... Pete Garret. Harper rolled those five names about in his mind methodically, just as he had done a thousand or more times while sweating out the hours inside Big Lonesome's repressive walls, recalling in detail their appearances, their characteristics and mannerisms, reviewing each carefully so that he would not forget even the smallest trait or idiosyncrasy.

They were the ones, in addition to the member of the gang he had killed—one Jim Rooney—who had cost him his star, his faith in the administration of the law, and thirty-one months of his life. They were outlaws, thieves, murderers, each one of them, and all deserving the gallows. Instead it had been he who had paid a penalty for the crime committed by them, while they had been set free to enjoy a share of the fifty thousand dollars in gold they had killed to get.

The money had belonged to a miner named Josh Moon. He and his wife, grubbing out a claim in the Colorado mountains, had, after twenty-five years, sold out to a syndicate that was circulating through the country buying up the successful small mines. With what the Moons had saved up over a quarter of a century and the amount they received from the syndicate, they had with them somewhere over fifty thousand dollars when they pulled out on their return trip to their original home in the east.

How Lavendar and the other members of his gang, all small-time, petty outlaws, learned of the fortune the Moons were carrying, Harper was never able to discover, but the fact was that they had.

Jake stirred on the saddle, shifted his weight to ease the pains in his back and legs; there'd been a time when he could ride all day, and the night if need be, and notice no discomfort, but all those months in Big Lonesome had changed that, softened him insofar as straddling a horse was concerned.

There had been nothing he could do about that during the tedious confinement, but maintaining skill in handling a pistol was a different matter. Purloining a knife soon after his term began, he surreptitiously carved from a block of wood a crude replica approximating the size and weight of the forty-five he'd left on deposit in the general store at Higgtown.

Once it was completed, he practiced daily when he was beyond the reach of the guard's attention, as well as at night during those hours when sleep would not come—which was only too often. He had always been expert with a sixgun, and while there was no way to judge accuracy, he felt certain he'd lost none of his speed, was possibly even faster than before.

His hand dropped to the weapon at his side. Whipping it out, he fired several quick shots at a nearby stump, hitting it successively but startling the gelding and sending him to shying briefly. Reloading, he examined the fresh cartridges. They were showing signs of corrosion. He'd best replace them at his first opportunity; better to discard them than chance a misfire at a critical moment.

Holstering the weapon, Jake twisted about, swept the rolling, grassy country that lay behind him with a sharp glance. There was no one on his trail. Caleb Lynch was a mite slow getting started if he planned to keep up. It could have been just talk, Harper thought, and then discarded the idea; Deputy Marshal Lynch had never been one for idle words.

Jake shifted his eyes to the north, to the towering Rocky Mountains that formed a ragged blue backdrop to the plains. Red Rock was in that direction, not far from where Josh Moon's gold mine lay. He'd been the town lawman there, and things had gone well. The settlement was busy, prosperous, and growing steadily. He'd had few problems except for a complaint now and then over his being a bit too strict. But that was what the majority of the people in Red Rock wanted, and he'd given it to them as best he knew how during the seven years he wore their badge.

It was for Red Rock that the Moons were heading with their treasure when the outlaws ambushed them. Being the nearest town where the couple could catch a stagecoach that would deliver them to the railroad, it was a natural choice.

Harper's jaw hardened as he recalled that warm fall day. It had been around midmorning. He was standing in the doorway to his office admiring the brilliant gold of the leaves clothing the cottonwoods in the grove below the settlement when Earl Petrie, a cowhand working for the Forked Lightning outfit, one of the nearby ranches, swung into the street and came pounding up on a lathered horse.

"Man and woman laying dead!" he'd shouted in a

rush of words as he came off his saddle. "Run across them while I was chousing strays. . . ."

"Where?" Jake had asked, trying to calm the rider.

"Below them bluffs—this side of Vipperman Peak."

Harper had called the local coroner, recruited two other men, a wagon, and with Petrie had gone immediately to the scene. The man, Josh Moon according to papers in his pockets, and his wife, Maude, had both been shot several times. The murder had occurred earlier that morning, the coroner figured.

Further perusal of Moon's papers revealed the sale of their mining property and indicated they were carrying a large sum of cash, probably intending to convert the money to a bank draft when they reached Red Rock before continuing their journey east. It was a case of robbery and murder, all had agreed.

The killers had left a trail. Six horses had moved away from the scene, striking southeast. Jake had set out to follow, while the others headed back to town with the bodies.

He'd had little difficulty in tracking the killers, who seemed to take no pains to hide their passage, and caught up with them in the settlement of Flintlock, some fifty miles below the buttes where the murders had taken place—finding all six horses drawn up behind a shack at the edge of the town.

Entering cautiously, Harper confronted the outlaws, all of whom he'd watched ride through Red Rock that previous day. They were lounging about in the one-room hut, four of them playing cards and drinking while the remaining two dozed in bunks.

All had come to attention when Jake stepped in. The youngest of the group, named Jim Rooney, Harper was to learn, had gone for his gun when he recognized the lawman. Jake downed him before he could get off a shot.

"Told you we'd never get away with killing them two!" Rooney had said as he lay dying. "That gold ain't going to do us no good now."

Jake had then taken the others into Flintlock and lodged them in the jail, charging them with robbery and murder. Each had protested he knew nothing of the crime, and a search of their persons and their gear failed to turn up the gold. Nor did a thorough going-over of the shack and its surrounding area. The outlaws had cached the money somewhere in the stretch of country lying between the hut and the buttes where the murder had been enacted.

But Jake Harper knew the men were guilty. He had Jim Rooney's dying words to back up his charge of murder, as well as the men from Red Rock who would testify that six horses had been ridden away from the area where Josh and Maude Moon's bodies were found.

It had all counted for nothing. Henry—Hank—Lavendar, who appeared to be the leader of the outlaws, engaged a clever lawyer to defend him and his friends, and the lawyer skillfully pointed out such deficiencies as the fact that no gold was ever found, that no witnesses actually saw any of his clients commit the murder or could testify they were even in that part of the country. All that was evident was that they had passed nearby.

As to Rooney's last words, there had been none. All five outlaws swore to that. Jake Harper, who was known to be a zealous lawman, had simply invented the statement to cover another fact—that he had needlessly shot down young Rooney in cold blood.

The trial before Circuit Judge Amos Chancellor,

with Deputy U.S. Marshal Caleb Lynch standing by, had taken a direct turnabout at that time. The attorney representing the outlaws had stressed the point that Harper was known to be a hard-nosed, unforgiving type of lawman who prided himself on never making a mistake, that he was acting out of his jurisdiction in that he was outside his own county, and that no concrete evidence against the five men he was defending had been produced.

Further, the only murder committed involving his clients was the one wherein Town Marshal Jake Harper had shot down young Jim Rooney in a fit of anger when he discovered the men had nothing to do with the killing of Josh Moon and his wife, Maude. Instead of his clients being declared guilty of murder and robbery, he asked for their acquittal and demanded that Jake Harper be charged with Rooney's killing.

The judge had agreed. All evidence indicated the validity of such, he stated. There was no gold, there were no witnesses to link the six men to the murders—only that they could have been in the vicinity, which they freely admitted. And a man named Jim Rooney had been shot to death by Marshal Harper, who did not deny it. As to Rooney's last words, five men swore under oath no such utterance was made, and it was not reasonable to assume that only Harper could have heard them; therefore it was only logical to believe that no such statement was ever made.

But Jake Harper, Judge Chancellor had noted, was a conscientious lawman, as the residents of Red Rock testified, if a bit on the zealous side. He evidently was performing what he believed to be his duty, and while the shooting of one Jim Rooney was uncalled for and unnecessary, it was understandable that in the heat of the moment, with one man standing up to six whom he doubtlessly believed to be killers, he would make use of his weapon.

The end result was that Henry Lavendar, Richter, Bannock, Matt Sandman, and Pete Garret were freed of all charges and Jake Harper, with due consideration for his record as a lawman, was sentenced to five years in prison for manslaughter.

Thus it had begun and ended; but for Jake Harper it was far from being over. Brushing at the sweat beading his forehead, he glanced at the sun, now well up in an empty, steel-blue sky. He'd start the search at Flint-lock. Perhaps one of the five outlaws would have settled there after the trial ended.

If not, his chances for finding out where they had gone would be better than elsewhere. One thing was certain—he would find them and exact the penalty from them that Judge Amos Chancellor had failed to assess. A one-man vigilante committee, Caleb Lynch had called him. All right. So be it.

4

Harper looked down upon Flintlock from a grove of trees that crowned a hill to the east of the settlement. The place had changed considerably. At the time of the trial it had been a fairly busy town—or so it had seemed to him then. Now its few buildings appeared gray, badly weathered, with their storefront signs faded and askew from the hammering of the winds, while an air of abandonment lay over all.

But it was not deserted entirely, Jake noted as he rode off the slope and drew nearer. A half-dozen horses stood at the hitchrack of the Forty-four Saloon, and he thought he could see someone in the general store. Puzzled, wondering, hopes sagging, he swung the black in beside the other mounts—likely the property of cowhands passing through and pausing for a drink—and dismounted. The chances he would find anyone in the settlement who knew Henry Lavendar and the other outlaws had dwindled suddenly. In all probability the people who were living in Flintlock during the trial had long since moved, forsaking the dying town for whatever reason had brought about its demise, and leaving it to strangers willing to take over their holdings at little or no cost.

Wrapping the black's reins about the crossbar, Harper stepped up onto the split-board landing of the saloon, and hesitated. Quiet, he let his eyes again run the rows of deserted buildings, remembering it as it had been, teeming with the excitement of the trial, the street crowded, the stores busy, smells and sounds of activity everywhere. That was only two and a half years ago—not long in the calculation of a lifetime; but towns rose swiftly, flourished, and died equally fast along the frontier, which was eternally changing.

Harper shifted his attention to his back trail, turning, his tall frame squared to the sunlight. A lean man just past thirty, he stood a full six feet in height and had the solid, muscular look of one accustomed to hardship. His dark hair hung thick to his collar, and the beard he now wore, to complement the full, curving moustache that had always graced his features, had a reddish tinge.

He'd taken care of himself while in Big Lonesome, making the best of the plain food and keeping fit by never shirking the harsh manual labor assigned to him and other convicts. He'd set his mind to that end long before the gates had closed behind him, for one day he would be free, and when that hour came, he wanted to be ready both physically and mentally.

There was no sign of Caleb Lynch on the trail. Shrugging indifferently, he lowered his gaze, allowed his eyes to settle again on the general store. He had been wrong; it was only a shell, and what he'd taken to be a man was only a plank leaning against a roof support. The dozen or so other structures were no different, even to the church. All were empty, element-scoured hulls, forlorn and forgotten in the bleaching sunlight.

Pivoting slowly, Jake crossed to the doorway of the

saloon and entered. The batwings, which had once swung freely as men came and went, were gone, replaced by crudely aligned planks that hung uneasily from hinges made of old harness leather.

A single lamp hung above a makeshift bar of unfinished lumber erected at the back of the room. Where before there had been a dozen or more tables with a quartet of chairs encircling each, there were now a few rough benches and tables improvised by sawing whiskey kegs to three-quarter height. Against the far side of the dimly lit area, several bunks had been constructed, making it apparent the Forty-four now offered lodging for the night, should a pilgrim desire to lay over.

Jake Harper glanced at the handful of men hunched around one of the tables where a game of cards was under way, and drew up to the bar. He nodded to the man standing behind it, a balding, unshaven individual in a collarless black shirt closed at the neck by a copper button, ragged checked vest, nondescript trousers. His round, red-veined face was not familiar.

"Whiskey," Harper said.

The barman reached for a glass, ran a finger about its interior to remove any dust, and poured it full from a bottle sitting on a wall shelf with several others where a back bar ordinarily would be.

"Drink's a quarter. . . ."

Jake drew a silver dollar from a pocket and laid it on the rough planks. Tossing off the whiskey, he gagged as the raw liquor burned a course down his throat.

"God in heaven, man, that's—"

The bartender's shoulders stirred. "Good liquor's hard to come by around here," he said. "Want another'n?"

Harper nodded, waited while his glass was refilled. A sudden burst of laughter came from the men engaged in the poker game, followed by a string of oaths voiced by one who evidently had been the butt of some sort of joke.

"Town's changed a mite," Jake said tentatively, toying with his glass. "Was a pretty lively town last time I was here."

The balding man bobbed, collected a second quarter from the change he'd laid on the counter. "Must've been a couple a years ago. . . ."

"More like three. What happened?"

"Changed the road. Folks're crossing farther west of here. Don't hardly nobody ever come this way nowadays. Cowhand or two once in a while."

"You living here when things were good?"

"Yeh. Worked in this here same saloon. Was the swamper. Name's Kallock—maybe you recollect me?"

Harper rubbed at his jaw. "Seems I do," he replied, hopeful of getting the man to open up more. "What happened to the fellow that owned the place then? Name was . . ."

"Avery. George Avery. He moved on, same as everybody else done when things went to hell. I stayed right here. Figured I could make as good a living running the place for myself as I could swamping in some other jasper's saloon."

"Do pretty good?"

"Well, me and my old woman ain't starving. Now and then rent out them bunks and serve up some chow, along with my whiskey. You looking for something to eat? Old woman's got antelope stew on the stove ready to dish up."

Harper shook his head. "Only eating twice a day anymore, so I'll wait for supper. Where'd Avery go?"

"Down Texas way—place called Corsicana. Town's really booming, we was told. Ever been there?"

"No, can't say as I have. . . . Couple others I recollect from when I was here—fellow named Lavendar. And there was another one, Denver Bannock."

Kallock pursed his lips, frowned. "Bannock I sure don't remember, but that other'n, Lavendar, he's running a hotel over in Oroville. Hear somebody mention him now and then."

Jake Harper had come to quiet attention. "You say Oroville?"

"Yeh, it's a couple a days' ride southwest. Ain't ever been there myself, but I been told it's a pretty fair-sized town."

Harper forced a smile. "Kind of a town Hank'd pick. Always was a lucky cuss."

"For sure—like that murder thing him and some others . . . Say, that fellow you mentioned, Bannock—I think he was one of them that was mixed up in it with him."

"Murder?" Jake repeated innocently.

"Yeh, him and three or four other jaspers got hauled up for killing some miner. Lawman that drug them into the judge claimed they'd robbed the fellow of a lot of gold, nigh onto a hundred thousand dollars' worth, I think it was, before they shot him. That sheriff or marshal, whichever he was, killed one of them bringing them in.

"Lavendar and them was all turned loose by the judge on account of the lawman couldn't prove nothing of what he claimed. Fact is, he got sent to the pen hisself for the killing he done. Was one of them trigger-happy badge-toters, seems, the kind that always figures they ain't never wrong."

"You know him?"

"Sure did. Was from some town north of here. Don't exactly recollect his name right at the moment, but he got what was coming to him. You want another drink?"

Harper, a bitter smile pulling at the corners of his mouth, laid a hand across his glass and shook his head. Two shots of what Kallock was passing off for whiskey was enough.

"Nope, riding on," he said, satisfaction running through him. He had the first of the outlaws—Henry Lavendar—located. Getting on their trail had been easier than he'd hoped.

"Which way you heading?"

"West. There a town I can reach by dark?"

Kallock gave that consideration. "Well, there ain't no town, but there's the Valley Stage Company's waystation. You'll hit it about then—being less'n thirty miles or so off."

He could reach the stage stop well before night if he wished, Jake realized, but it didn't really matter; he knew where he was to go—a town called Oroville. It would be a good idea to lay over at the waystation, get some food in his belly, and enjoy a comfortable night's rest before riding on to face Lavendar.

Picking up his change, he nodded to the saloon keeper. "Obliged to you for talking. Like as not I'll drop back by again someday."

"Expect you'll find me right here," Kallock said cheerfully. "Too dang poor to move on. . . . Good luck."

"Thanks, and same to you," Harper said, and turned for the doorway.

Deputy Marshall Caleb Lynch halted in the trees outside Flintlock and studied the lone survivor of the once-busy settlement—the Forty-four Saloon. He could see the hitchrack from where he sat astride his sorrel, and there were no horses drawn up to it. But Jake Harper was there, or had been there, he was dead certain.

Flintlock would be the first town he'd line out for, it being the place where Henry Lavendar and the rest of his bunch had last been before he'd taken Harper off to prison. Going there would do Jake little good, however. Buck Kallock wouldn't be able to tell him much about the gang, if anything at all. Buck'd been George Avery's swamper at the time the trial was being held, and was probably never sober enough to take note of anything.

But he'd best swing by and do a little jawing with Buck, see if Harper was still around or if he'd learned anything that would be of help to him. That meant buying at least one drink of that God-awful rotgut Kallock served up as whiskey—he'd never get anything out of the man otherwise—but it was necessary. He needed to be sure he was on Harper's trail. That damned puncher he'd gotten sidetracked to and followed after leaving Higgtown had cost him several hours before he woke up to the fact that he was tailing the wrong black horse.

The old lawman glared at the sun, now low in the sky and not too far from the horizon. He'd be sleeping under a cedar that night most likely, he thought angrily as he started down the grade, and goddamnit, he was getting too old for that! But it would be worth it if it enabled him to put Jake Harper back in Big Lonesome where he belonged.

~⟨ 5 ⟩~

A curious sort of ease settled over Harper as he mounted his horse and struck out across the rolling plains to the west of Flintlock. For the first time the hard, brittle tension that had been a part of his being all those many months began to taper off, and the cool, quiet serenity that had manifested his way of life prior to the years in prison took over.

Perhaps it was that he finally was realizing he was again a free man, no longer a captive within the walls of forbidding Big Lonesome; or possibly it was the knowledge that he had so quickly crossed the trail of the outlaws whom he'd set out to find—or at least one of them, Henry Lavendar. And locating Lavendar would surely lead to the others.

Pulling off his hat, Jake brushed at the sweat on his forehead with the back of a hand. He grinned, eyes pausing on the limp-brimmed, considerably battered piece of headgear. It showed the years of service it had rendered; he hadn't noticed how bad a condition it was in.

At the first town he reached he'd outfit himself completely—new hat, shirt, pants, even boots. His feet felt a bit cramped in the pair he was wearing. All of his clothing had been laid aside for prison garb when he'd entered Big Lonesome, to be reclaimed when he was released, and all except the boots had fit fairly well. But like the hat, he reckoned everything should be replaced. No point in giving folks the idea he was a down-at-the-heel drifter.

And spurs—he needed a pair. The ones he'd turned over to the prison custodian with the rest of his clothing were missing when the time came to reclaim his possessions. None of Big Lonesome's officials could account for their disappearance, but the fact remained that they were gone. It was no great loss, and easily replaced, so Harper had made no issue of it.

Had it been his gun—a finely tuned Colt forty-five with silk-smooth action and weighted to give perfect balance—it would have been a different matter. He was glad he'd left the weapon with his money at the store depository in Higgtown; its loss would have been irreplaceable.

He must remember to follow his earlier decision and buy fresh cartridges for the pistol. True, there'd been no misfires when he'd limbered up the weapon after leaving Higgtown, but he'd been a fool to take chances. He should pick himself up a rifle, too, and a belt knife. There were times when a long gun and a sharp blade came in handy.

Twisting about, Harper looked back. Still no sign of Caleb Lynch. The lawman had either lost the trail or had not planned to follow him after all. Possibly he intended to do so later. And it could be that Lynch knew that Henry Lavendar was to be found in Oroville and was riding straight to the settlement, not wasting time on tracking. If so, would he warn the outlaw?

Harper shrugged. Let him. It would change nothing other than put Lavendar, now apparently passing himself off as a respectable businessman, on his guard. Henry Lavendar and all the others—Bannock, Richter, Garret, and Sandman—would have to face him eventually.

Changing position, throwing his weight to one leg in an effort to ease his aching muscles, Jake allowed his gaze to reach out across the land unrolling before him. The flat he was crossing was green with late-spring grass, and the slopes beyond the buttes rising on both his left and right were studded with rabbitbush, bayonet yucca, and bright with patches of yellow flowers. Thinly scattered cedars marked the countryside, which was gradually breaking up into washes and wide, sandy-bottomed arroyos.

Twice he saw coveys of quail, disturbed by the approach of the gelding and sent scurrying off into the shelter of nearby brush, and once he came upon a pair of coyotes quarreling over a rabbit. Both slunk quickly off into the weed-filled depths of a draw until he had passed to a safe distance, and then hurriedly returned to their prize. A light wind was fanning his face as he rode, and thus he had been able to approach the lean, wary little prairie wolves from below; otherwise they would have caught his scent and been gone long before he saw them.

Far ahead a thin wisp of smoke hung in the cloudless sky. It would be coming from the waystation, he reckoned—likely only another half-hour or so in the distance. Jake stirred, shifted his weight to the opposite leg. He should be able to get that good meal he was needing there, and hopefully, a bed. Too bad it was to be only a stage stopover and not a town he would be reaching; he could then do the buying he had in mind and have done with it.

A night's rest would serve him well, one attained on

something other than the iron cots and thin pads of Big Lonesome. The change in food, too—from prison fare to something more solid and substantial—would be most welcome, although eating had never held much meaning to him other than being a necessity to sustain life and strength. He ate what was served up to him wherever he might be, or if on the trail, made do with what was in his grub sack.

The land began to rise gently, lift toward a range of blue-gray mountains now taking ragged shape along the southwestern horizon. The Capulins, he seemed to recall their being named, but he wasn't sure. It had been a while since he was in the area, and it could be he was yet too far north for that particular string of hills.

The slope topped out on a high mesa, flattened into a wide, near-level plain splattered with cholla cactus and countless round clumps of snakeweed. A row of low-roofed buildings stood in bleak solitude in the distance, all appearing soft-edged and gently blurred in their remoteness. The waystation, Harper realized, and put the black to a lope.

A coach with a four-horse hitch stood in front of the largest of the buildings. Beyond it Jake could see the corral where the spare animals were kept, the barn that housed feed and extra gear. A water trough with a pitcher pump, a hitchrack, and several split-log benches were placed conveniently about in the area adjacent to the station's entrance.

Harper swung onto the well-defined road a short distance above the stage stop and came onto it from its windowless north side. As he drew near, the driver of the coach emerged from the station, and placing a foot on the hub of a front wheel, began to climb up to his high seat. Passengers began to appear: a woman, well-dressed in eastern fashion; a drummer carrying some sort of leather sample case; and a small, wiry man in striped gray suit and narrow-brimmed felt hat who moved with an easy, offhand insolence.

Harper's eyes narrowed. There was something familiar to the latter passenger, something that struck a chord and aroused a wariness within him. He drummed at the black's ribs with his heels, cursing his lack of spurs, endeavored to reach the station before the coach pulled out. He was too late. The big Concord, dipping and rocking as it got under way, whirled out onto the road and quickly gained speed on the grade south of the station.

Harper drew up to the water trough, dismounted, his glance on the coach now vanishing in a swirl of dust. He'd known the man in the felt hat from somewhere, he was certain, but too much distance had separated them to afford a good look. Likely it was someone from Red Rock.

Allowing the black a brief drink, he moved on to the rack, slip-knotted the reins about the crossbar, and walked stiffly, favoring his muscles, to the station's entrance. Pulling back the screen door, he entered. An elderly man was bending over a long table covered by a red-and-white-checked cloth collecting empty coffeecups. Two other men—hostlers, to judge from their clothing—were slouched in chairs nearby. All glanced up.

The oldster at the table, evidently in charge of the waystation, paused. "Yeh?"

"Looking for a meal, and maybe a bed."

The man nodded. "Reckon I can take care of both. Thought maybe you was wanting to catch the stage. You'd be too late if you was. Just pulled out. Set down, and I'll bring you some victuals."

Harper settled onto a chair, glanced casually about at the collection of deer antlers nailed to the walls. "Where was that stage heading?"

"South. Connects with the El Paso line. Why?"

Jake shrugged. It felt good to be out of the saddle. "No reason. Thought I recognized one of the passengers, the one in the gray suit and politician's hat."

"I feed them and sometimes bed them down," the station manager said, turning away. "Don't never bother to find out who they are."

One of the hostlers shifted the cud of tobacco in his mouth, leaned forward. "You talking about the one that climbed aboard last?"

"Was a woman, a drummer, and him."

The hostler looked aside, accurately made a liquid deposit in a brass gaboon. "I know him," he said, facing Harper again. "Gambler. Seen him over in Lambert's Saloon in Cimarron a coupla weeks ago. Regular high-roller, I was told, and a mighty fancy dresser. I'll bet that there suit he was wearing cost maybe fifty dollars!"

"Happen to remember his name?" Jake asked, and shifted his attention to the station manager, coming through a doorway in the back of the room, a cup of coffee in one hand, a plate of food in the other.

"Yeh, sure do," the hostler said. "Richter. Yancey Richter's what they called him."

⌒ 6 ⌒

Richter. . . .

Coldness flooded through Jake Harper. He was barely conscious of picking up the cup of steaming black coffee, holding it to his lips, and taking a long drink.

"That who you thought it was?" the hostler wondered.

Jake set the cup back on the table and came to his feet. Reaching into a pocket, he dropped a silver dollar beside the untouched plate of food.

"Where's that stage stop next?"

"Oroville," the station man replied, frowning. "If you're wanting to catch up, you can cut across the mesa, head it off this side of the buttes. Ain't you going to eat your grub?"

"Maybe later," Harper said, and wheeling, crossed to the door.

Stepping out into the open, he reached the black in a half-dozen long strides, jerked the leathers free, and swung onto the saddle. There was a hurried but studied manner to his movements, wholly devoid of all wasted motion, and within only moments he was cutting away from the road below the waystation and angling toward a line of dark-faced bluffs he could see in the west.

The road, he supposed, circled wide to avoid the deep arroyo he shortly encountered. Guiding the gelding down into it and across to the opposite side, he put the big horse to a fast gallop, aiming for a point near the end of the buttes, where, logically, the road would veer back to resume its direct course.

The black, running free over the flat land, covered the distance in good time, and dropping off a low hill not many minutes later, Harper rejoined the established course. He was there ahead of the stagecoach only briefly, for as he drew off to one side he could hear the steady pound of the horses' hooves and the grating of the vehicle's iron-tired wheels.

Cool, mind set dead-center on what he must do in the coming moments, Jake Harper waited. When the lead horses broke into view around the slight bend above him, he urged the gelding out until he was in the middle of the dual ruts. Drawing his gun, he raised it as a signal for the driver to stop.

The man on the box, a grizzled oldster with a flowing white moustache and small black eyes, hauled back on the lines and threw on the brake. Harper, not changing position, which offered no target to either of the men inside the coach, watched silently until the plunging team had settled down, and then moved in closer, still keeping the span in front of him. The driver, eyes snapping, face angry, came to his feet.

"What the hell's the matter with you? This here stage don't carry no strongbox—nothing but passengers."

"That's what I'm interested in," Harper replied calmly. "Throw that gun you're wearing off to the side and set down. Nothing for you to worry about."

The driver complied impatiently, turning his head slightly to call out to his fares: "It's all right, folks. Just do what you're told."

Harper waited until the old man had resumed his seat, and then he guided the black up to the flank of the restless team.

"Everybody out," he ordered.

The door opened immediately, and the drummer, placing a foot on the step, appeared. He looked at Harper anxiously, hastily completed his dismount, and took up a stand by the rear wheel of the dust-covered vehicle.

The woman came next. Somewhere in her late twenties, Jake supposed, she was trim and attractive in a light blue traveling suit and a small feathered hat that was tilted forward on her head. She had dark hair, a fair skin only beginning to be discolored by the hot sun, and steady blue eyes that were brimming with indignation as she halted near the drummer.

"This is an outrage!" she fumed. "I intend to see that something is done about this!"

Harper barely heard. His glance, narrowed by suspicion, had not strayed from the doorway of the coach. The last passenger, the gambler, was slow in getting out. Had Yancey recognized him and was attempting to make an escape through the door on the opposite side of the Concord, or was he endeavoring to get a bead on him from the open window?

"Richter!" he snapped, coming off the black fast. "Come out of there!"

The gambler appeared at that moment, dropping lightly to the ground without bothering to use the metal step. He considered Jake slyly.

"I know you?"

"Name's Harper."

The outlaw hung motionless for several long moments and then slowly straightened. "That there lawman—"

"Right," Jake cut in coldly, stepping away from his horse to where he was fully in the open. "I'm here to finish what the law started."

Richter squared himself, his narrow features taut. He wore an ornately tooled cartridge belt under his coat, and now, moving deliberately, brushed the front of the garment back to where the pistol hanging at his hip was more available.

"Figured you was still in the pen," he said, his voice low and almost conversational.

"That judge's conscience got the best of him, it seems. Knew you and the others were guilty all the time, so he tried to make up for what he did."

"You a lawman?" the drummer asked nervously.

Harper shook his head.

"Then why're you—"

"Keep out of this!" Jake snarled. "Don't concern you."

The girl stared at him, shock and disbelief on her smooth features. "You . . . you're not going to kill him!" she protested in a strangled voice.

Harper, never for the briefest moment taking his eyes off the outlaw, said, "Best you get back inside the stage, lady."

"No, I won't! I'll . . ."

Jake did not hear, had dismissed the girl from his mind, his thoughts concentrating wholly on the man facing him.

"When you're ready, Richter . . ."

The gambler moved his head slowly from side to side. "You're loco—plumb loco," he murmured. "And I ain't about to draw on you. I'm remembering you good now, and how fast you are with that iron you're packing."

"You're forgetting I've been in the pen for a couple of years and more. Ought to make us about even."

"Maybe," Richter said, and let his coat fall forward and cover his holstered pistol. "I ain't about to find out. You shoot me, it'll have to be in the back."

Yancey Richter started to turn away. Abruptly his arm came up. Sunlight glinted on metal as the smaller weapon secreted in his coat sleeve popped into his hand.

Harper drew and fired in a single, flowing motion. In that same fragment of time the outlaw also triggered his weapon, and the two reports blended, almost into one, bringing a shrill scream to the lips of the girl and startling the restless horses.

Motionless, Jake Harper watched Richter sink slowly to the ground, the hideout pistol he grasped falling from his stiffening fingers. Then, crossing to the sprawled figure of the outlaw, he reached down, felt for a pulse. There was none. Stepping back, Jake motioned to the coach driver.

"Load him up. Can drop him at your next stop."

The old man came off his perch quickly, voicing no comment, and ducking his head at the drummer, moved to where the outlaw lay. Features grim and cold, Harper watched them pick up the lifeless body, place it in the boot of the coach after first making room for it by removing several metal suitcases and a carpetbag, which they tossed up onto the vehicle's roof.

Harper, under the abhorring stare of the girl, reloaded his weapon, dropped it back into the holster. Then, turning his attention to her, he nodded slightly.

"Sorry you had to see that."

"Sorry!" she echoed. "You've just shot a man down, killed him, and all you can say is you're sorry!"

He shook his head coldly. "Don't get me wrong. Not sorry for that—only that you saw it. He's had it coming for a long time."

"But you had no right—"

"Had every right, lady," Jake cut in harshly, and turned to face the old driver standing respectfully off to one side. "Yeh?"

"It all right if I get along? Running late now, this here stopping while—"

"Go ahead," Harper replied.

The driver wheeled about, gestured to his passengers as he hurriedly climbed to his seat. "Get aboard, folks," he said urgently. "We're moving out."

The drummer pushed by the girl, climbed quickly into the coach. Harper stepped up to her side, offered his hand. She scoured him with a hating look, shook him off, and drew herself inside. Jake shrugged, closed the door, and stepped back.

"I'm reporting this murder to the first sheriff we see," the girl called to him through the open window. "I've had a good look at you, so I can give him a full description."

Harper smiled wearily. "Reckon that's your right, lady," he said, and turned to his horse.

~ 7 ~

Seera settled back on the seat, the slightly mocking words of the hard-faced man who had just killed her ertswhile fellow passenger echoing in her ears. Then, leaning forward, gripping the windowsill to brace herself against the swaying of the coach as it got under way, she threw a final glance at him. Face tipped down, he was walking slowly through the streaming sunlight to his horse. What was he thinking? Was he regretting his murderous act?

He should be, she thought, again sliding back on the worn seat cushion. It was unbelievable, horrible! There surely must be some sort of law to protect a person from killers like that, even in this godforsaken country! After all, the Territory of New Mexico was a part of the United States!

"Was a terrible thing for you to see. . . ."

She raised her eyes to the man sitting across from her. He had endeavored to start a conversation with her earlier, shortly after he'd gotten aboard at one of the several stops the stage had made along the way. He was a sales representative from New York, he'd said, and introduced himself as K. C. Kunkle—Casey to his friends.

She'd responded coolly, as she'd been taught as a child to do when accosted by a stranger, and he'd let it drop. He had tried again when the man who'd been killed became a passenger, but she'd again disdained his overtures, and thereafter he'd confined his attention to the newcomer—Richter, the outlaw who'd shot him down had called him. Now anger and indignation had ruptured the barriers carried over from childhood, and she felt the need to talk, vent her feelings.

"How can a thing like that happen?" she demanded, as the coach, having gained full speed, rushed on through the warm day. "It's . . . it's uncivilized!"

"You'll find things a bit different out here," Kunkle said. "Ain't no policeman standing on every corner like there probably was where you came from, Miss . . ."

"Lavendar . . . Seera Lavendar."

"Thank you. I'm Casey Kunkle . . . but I think I mentioned that. Anyway, as I said, there're no policemen handy out here, and men settle their differences with guns. Where is your home?"

"Pittsburgh, in Pennsylvania. I was born in Nebraska, but after my mother died, my father sent me to live with his sister and her family in Pittsburgh."

"New York's where I hail from, but I've traveled this country a lot. Did you say your name was Lavendar?"

"Yes."

"You happen to be any relation to Henry Lavendar, the fellow that runs the Cattleman's Hotel in Oroville?"

The girl nodded. "Yes, he was my father. I'm going—"

"Was?" the drummer interrupted, frowning.

"He was shot and killed about two weeks ago—murdered like that man back there."

Kunkle leaned back, shook his head. "Mighty sorry to hear that. Stayed at his place last time I was in Oroville—about a year or so ago, I guess it was. He was a fine gentleman. Do you know what happened?"

Seera stirred, tightened her grip on the windowsill as the stage plunged down into a dip, thundered up the opposite side, creaking and popping noisily.

"Only what Sheriff Dakin said in the letter he wrote to me—that my father had been shot. He didn't know who had done it, but was investigating. . . . It would be some murderer like that man back there—Harper, I think his name is."

"Maybe. It sounded to me like there was some long-standing argument between him and Richter, however, something that happened years ago, concerning the law. This Richter looked like a gambler to me, and he tried to trick the other fellow with a gun he had up his sleeve."

"Doesn't change anything. It was still murder."

"Folks out here won't look on it that way. Richter was given a fair chance to draw his pistol and shoot it out. Instead he made like he wasn't going to accept the challenge, and then tried to fool the tall fellow."

Seera Lavendar shuddered. "No matter how you try to explain it or justify it, it was murder."

Kunkle smiled. "Not trying to justify it, just hoping to show you how things are out here. I know how you feel. Hit me the same way when I made my first trip into this part of the country six years ago. I had a hard time getting used to how people live and do things, but I did. You will, too—if you stay."

"I plan to," the girl said, gaze on a distant row of ragged buttes. Through the sunlight-shot dust stirred up by the horses' hooves and the spinning wheels, the formations appeared to be of gold.

"In Oroville?"

Seera nodded. *Where else?* She was twenty-four years old, unmarried, and destined to a life as an old-maid schoolteacher insofar as Pittsburgh was concerned—a future that had no appeal. The aunt and uncle who had reared her were well up in years and several times had made it evident they wished she would strike out on her own.

When that became apparent to her, she had cast about for a new life, one that would hold some interest; as if in answer to her desire, the letter from Sheriff Jess Dakin in a far-off town called Oroville had arrived, advising her of the death of her father and that she was now the owner of a hotel.

Being the mistress of a hotel in some distant western settlement wasn't exactly her idea of a future; her thoughts had run more to the big cities in the east, where she might find a well-paying job, or at least one that would afford her a comfortable living. Inquiries, however, had brought few responses, most of which pointed out that times were hard, and openings for women were practically nonexistent, even as a schoolteacher, which she definitely did not plan to continue being.

Word from the sheriff of Oroville, a town somewhere in New Mexico, relative to her father's death had come not so much as a shock but as a surprise. During the nineteen years she'd lived with her aunt and uncle, she had heard from her parent exactly six times—all brief notes containing a small amount of money for her upkeep.

She had lost her mother while they were living on a Nebraska homestead, and her dying had made a different man of her father apparently. Actually, she could recall very little about him, but he had evidently changed from the hard-working man she vaguely recalled who left their one-room soddy at daybreak to stumble back in at dark, tired and irritable and uncommunicative, to one that cut all ties and knocked about the country in aimless fashion, doing little and never staying in one place for long.

Seera wished she might have known her father better, but he seemed to have little interest in her or her well-being. His letters had been no more than notes, were always devoid of affection, and seemed to be more in the line of duty than anything else. And the money he enclosed was always but a small amount and fell far short of being sufficient to supply her needs.

The row of cliffs—buttes, she remembered hearing Casey Kunkle call them—had slanted down to merge with the sameness of the land across which they were moving. A blur of color caught her eye, and she bent toward the window for a better look through the yellowish haze. . . . Some sort of animal—tan and white—racing for another line of hills farther off. There were two dozen or more in the group.

"Antelope," Kunkle said, noting her interest. "There's a lot of them around here. Fact is, a plenty of the restaurants serve them on their bill of fare and try to pass the meat off as venison, or even beef. But you can tell the difference. Meat's strong, smells like mutton."

Seera smiled, resumed her position designed to coincide with the motions of the coach. A low thud came from the baggage compartment behind her as a wheel struck a chuckhole with solid force. She shuddered. It would be the body of the dead man—Richter—jostling about. Vaguely she heard the drummer's voice again, barely audible above the noise of the stage-coach.

"I . . . I beg your pardon . . ."

Kunkle smiled, brushed at his mouth with a handkerchief. "I was asking if you were married."

"No."

"A widow, perhaps?"

Kunkle was basing his questions on her appearance, Seera realized. By all rights, a girl—woman, really—of the age she was should have or have had a husband.

"I've never been married."

The drummer laughed, slapped his knee. "By Christopher, the boys in Pittsburgh must've been blind or mighty bashful, letting an attractive girl like you get away!"

It was meant as a compliment, but that didn't blunt the sting to any degree. Seera smiled dutifully. "Thank you. It's just that I've never had the inclination."

"Never met the right man is what I expect you mean," Kunkle said. "Well, that's the best way to be. Marriage is a long-time thing, I always say, and folks ought to be sure before they take the step. I'm in the same boat myself. Just never found the right woman."

"Likely you will someday."

"Sure not holding my breath till I do," the drummer said, winking and smiling broadly. "You say you plan to stay in Oroville; that mean you're going to take over your pa's—father's—hotel, or do you plan to sell it?"

"I haven't actually made up my mind," Seera replied, brushing at the filmy dust settling on her face. "Not sure I can live in a country like this. It's so bleak, so cruel . . . and ugly."

The drummer glanced out of the window at the landscape racing by. "Yeh, guess it does look that way to someone coming here from one of the states where everything's covered with grass and trees. But you grow to like it, even see a sort of beauty in it."

Seera Lavendar sighed. "I'm afraid that will never happen to me. I see only emptiness and ragged rocks and miles and miles of nothing except things that look like starved weeds. Add all that to the kind of rough people you find—"

"Wait," Kunkle broke in gently. "Give things a chance before you decide to give up."

She smiled wryly, listening briefly to the shouts of the driver floating back to them faintly. "I . . . I guess I don't have much choice—at least for a while."

"That's all it'll take—a little while, I'll bet. You saw a sample of the hard side of the country and the way folks do. There's plenty about it that's good. People live in nice houses in fine little towns, have children, and go to church. They work in stores and offices, or maybe they have a ranch or a farm, and they have good friends.

"And now and then actors from New York stop by and put on shows—why, I watched Eddie Foy not too long ago when I was in Dodge City. There's opera, too, in some of the bigger settlements, if that's what you like."

"I'm not too interested—in the vaudeville shows, either."

"Well, we have it all in this part of the country, too," the drummer said, his voice falling a bit. "Point I'm trying to make is that we're not totally uncivilized."

"We?" she echoed, smiling. "I thought you said you were a New Yorker."

"I am, but I guess the west has sort of gotten into my blood. If I ever get the chance, I aim to settle out here for good, maybe open up a little store of some kind."

Seera smiled again. "Would you be interested in buying a hotel?"

"Afraid not," he said with a laugh. "That's a bit out of my line, and I'd sure not want to go broke."

"Expect you know as much about running one as I do—more, likely."

"Possibly, but you'll be starting with nothing out of pocket. I'd have to lay out a lot of cash. . . . Like for you to know this, however. I'll be staying at your place, and if there's anything I can do in helping you get started—anything, mind you—you only have to speak up."

"Thank you," the girl said, attention once more on the world outside the stagecoach window. "How much longer will it be before we reach Oroville?"

Casey Kunkle consulted his thick, nickeled watch. "About two more hours."

Two hours, Seera thought. Two hours, and a new way of life for her would begin—if she so wished.

8

There was no glow of satisfaction coursing through Jake Harper as he swung up onto the black gelding and settled himself on the saddle. Rather, it was a sense of accomplishment, of fulfillment. A lawman through and through, he took no pleasure in putting an end to the life of any man, killer or otherwise, considered it only in the light of a job that had to be done.

For a time he continued to sit motionless on his horse, unseeing eyes fixed on the dust cloud surrounding the vanishing stagecoach, while the hard, bright tension drained from him, and then finally he clucked the black into an easy trot and moved on down the roadway.

It had occurred to Harper that the next stop the stage would make was likely Oroville—the town where Henry Lavendar reportedly lived. Assuming Caleb Lynch was not already there and had warned the outlaw, word of Yancey Richter's death would reach him quickly upon the arrival of the coach, and with it, not only a complete account of what had taken place but also a positive identification of the man who had slain the gambler.

Would Lavendar remember him? Would the name

Harper jog his memory, make him recall the lawman who had tracked down him and his partners, but who had himself gone to prison when their lies had prevailed over the truth? Most likely. Yancey Richter had remembered, and there was no reason to think that Henry Lavendar, who was the leader of the outlaw gang, would not, and immediately take precautions.

Mulling it over as he rode on through the hot sunshine, Harper concluded it would make no difference. Lavendar probably would turn to Oroville's lawman, seek his protection; he could call upon a close friend, possibly one or more of the original outlaw party if they were there, to back him; he could attempt his own defense. Or he could run.

Which ever, it would change nothing. Like some kind of grim avenger, he'd seek out Lavendar, force him into a shootout, and kill him just as he had Yancey Richter, and would do the same to the remainder of the outlaws. The prestige of the law would have then been upheld and the invincibility of justice proven.

Therefore there was no need to hurry, reach Oroville ahead of the stagecoach. In fact, it would be better to hold off, take his time getting to the settlement, and let Henry Lavendar sweat a little. As well drop back to the waystation, eat the meal he'd left on the table, and enjoy a night's rest in a comfortable bed.

Harper drew the black to a halt as he started to wheel and begin the return trip. Smoke hanging in the afternoon sky a distance to the east had caught his attention. He studied it intently for a long minute. It would be a town, he decided; there was not enough for a grass fire, too much for a rancher's kitchen chimney. At once he put the gelding to a lope for the dirty gray smudge, abandoning his thoughts of backtracking to the waystation; at a settlement he not only could find a place to eat and sleep but also purchase the items he felt he needed.

It was near dark when he turned into the main and only street of the town—Wolf's Crossing, a sign at a fork in the road had informed him. It was a small settlement, about the size that Flintlock had been, and was strung out along the banks of a clear, fast-flowing stream.

As he rode up to the largest of a dozen or so structures, one bearing the sign ROOMS TO LET, a tall young man wearing a star appeared in the doorway of the marshal's office. He hesitated briefly, then, stepping down into the loose dust, came forward.

Harper, off the gelding and in the process of winding the reins around the crossbar of the hitchrack, looked up, temper lifting swiftly.

"Howdy," the lawman said unsmilingly. "Ain't seen you around here before."

"First time," Jake replied quietly.

"Just riding through?"

Harper, a natural resentment of authority—born of the endless restrictive months in prison under the captious eyes of ever-present guards—still very much a part of his being, stiffened perceptibly as he looked the man up and down.

His anger ebbed. The deputy was little more than a boy, likely had been wearing his star for only a short while, and the cynicism that came with experience had yet to set in. Memories of his own early days as a lawman stirred through Jake Harper. He'd been like the young lawman once—eager, anxious to please, to do a good job of keeping his town clean and free of trouble.

"About it. Looking for a square meal, a bed, and a general store."

The deputy nodded briskly. "We got them all, and you're welcome here long as you behave."

"I'll be gone come sunup," Harper said.

The clean-shaven young lawman, brown eyes reflecting his friendliness, smiled. "Ain't running you out. Want you to know that, just that it's my job to keep tally on strangers. . . . You're looking for a place to sleep, this here one's about the best. Restaurant's down the street a piece—Ma Ferguson's. General store's back there on the corner."

"Livery stable?"

"Round behind the hotel."

"Obliged to you, deputy," Jake said, and stepping up onto the landing of the rooming house, entered.

The clerk of the hostelry, evidently once a private residence converted to accommodate travelers, was elderly and had difficulty in hearing. But Harper succeeded in making his needs known, and shortly was conducted to a room in the rear of the house after paying the necessary dollar and a half in advance—usual, he was informed, when a lodger had no baggage to indicate he was more than just a drifter.

That much accomplished, Harper stabled the black, and after giving instructions as to his care, sought out Ma Ferguson's restaurant. He was feeling the weight of weariness and the pain of muscles unused to hours in the saddle by that hour. The thought of a good bed awaiting him was most appealing.

But he held off, first having a meal of fried meat, potatoes, hot biscuits, and coffee, topped off with a wedge of dried-apple pie. When that was over, he made his way to the general store.

He took considerable time there, outfitting himself with a complete change of clothing, purchasing fresh ammunition for the pistol he carried, a pair of saddlebags, and a small supply of trail grub and the necessary utensils for making use of it.

Returning to his room, he left all but his new clothing and doubled back to the barber shop he'd noticed near the restaurant, which offered, besides the usual tonsorial attention, hot tub baths. When he emerged from the shop a bit later, he not only looked but felt like a changed man—barbered, bathed, and clad in new boots, cord pants, dark blue shield shirt, leather vest, and fawn-colored flat-crowned hat.

For the first day since entering Big Lonesome he had the feeling of being really clean, and that, allied with his new apparel, gave a lift to his spirits. It was as if he were starting life over again, and he reckoned he was, except for the duty that lay ahead of him—that of completing the task he'd taken upon himself. That was of the past, and there could be no new life for him until he had discharged what, to his literal mind, was a sacred if grim obligation.

Darkness had fallen by the time the renovation was finished, and now at ease and seeing the lights of a saloon at the lower end of the town, he moved for it, nodding casually to the greetings of several Wolf's Crossing residents as he passed along the board sidewalk.

There were only a dozen patrons inside the small narrow building as he entered, and stepping up to the bar, he called for a bottle of the establishment's best whiskey and a glass, paid, and withdrew to a table in a back corner. At once a fairly young woman separated herself from a group of men at the end of the counter and joined him.

"Looking for company, mister?" she asked, pushing a straying lock of dark hair back into place.

Harper shrugged, studied her briefly. She was a handsome woman despite the heavy application of cosmetics to her face.

"Get yourself a glass and sit down," he said.

The girl crossed languidly to the bar, returned, and settled onto the chair opposite him. "Friends call me Tildy. What's your name?" she asked, sliding her glass toward the bottle.

"Jake'll do," Harper replied, and filled the thick-bottomed container. Taking up his own, he murmured, *"Salud,"* and drained it.

Tildy downed her portion, nodded appreciatively. "See you bought yourself some of Gabe's best liquor. Don't happen around here very often."

It was good whiskey, erased the still-lingering recollection of the rotgut he'd tasted in Flintlock.

"Man needing a drink for a long time wants the best," he said, and again filled the glasses. Glancing about the saloon, a one-story affair devoid of rooms, he added, "You live around here close?"

"Out in back," Tildy said. "Got a place there. You aiming to be in town for long?"

"Leaving at first light."

"Hate to hear that," the girl murmured, tossing off her drink and setting her empty glass on the table. "Was hoping you'd gone to work somewheres around here."

Warmed by the liquor, Harper smiled genially. "Might be a real good idea, if I didn't have some personal business that needs looking after."

"Where?"

"Oroville."

Tildy sighed regretfully. "That's a long ways from

here." Then, "If you ain't going till morning, we still got tonight. . . ."

The glow engendered by the liquor, the pleasant smells and friendly sounds of the saloon, and the nearness of the girl—he'd all but forgotten what it was like to be around a woman during his stay in prison—combined to break the last taut restraints that shackled Jake Harper to purpose, at least for time present.

"That's a fact," he said, gathering up the glasses and bottle of whiskey and coming to his feet. "Lead the way."

⌐ 9 ⌐

Oroville. A small, grassy, tree-shaded area that lay near the exact center of a broad flat, the outgrowth and further extension of a spring that pushed its clear, cold water upward to form a lake.

Halting at the eastern edge of the settlement, Jake Harper swept the twin rows of false-fronted buildings standing shoulder to shoulder in mutual support along its main street. The Maricopa Saloon . . . Bill Williams' Livery Stable . . . Mason's Hay & Grain & Feed . . . The Emporium . . . Kansas Pride Restaurant, the upper floor of which apparently served as a meeting place for the Masonic and Knights of Pythias lodges . . . First Christian Church . . . Bibo's Bakery . . . Parsons' Gun Shop, and across from it, the Cattleman's Hotel.

Harper's drifting gaze came to a stop there, interest in the remaining business houses and residential section that lay back and away from the street gone. Eyes narrowing slightly, he considered the hostelry. A large, two-floored frame structure with sturdy carved posts supporting the roof shading its wide front gallery, it appeared prosperous and well-kept. Henry Lavendar

60

had made good use of his share of Josh Moon's gold, that was evident.

Jake's gaze paused on a small sign extending from a corner of the building. STAGECOACH OFFICE, it read. He smiled tightly. If there had been any doubt in his mind that Lavendar would be unaware of his coming, that was now dispelled. In all likelihood Yancey Richter's body had been unloaded at the hotel.

Features cold, Harper brought his attention back to the street, to the half-dozen persons moving along the board sidewalks, settled it finally on the squat structure that housed the jail and office of the local lawman. A sheriff, he noted. Oroville was evidently the county seat.

He could see no one either in or around the building, set back and a bit apart from its neighbors, guessed Lavendar had not alerted the lawman to his coming, or else all precautions taken were being kept undercover. Jake gave the latter thought, decided such was probably true; but the game could be played by both sides, and cutting the gelding around, he avoided openly entering the town by circling and coming into it from behind the structures on the west.

There, following the irregular, littered course of an alley, he rode to the rear of the hotel. Drawing up to the hitchrack, Harper dismounted, the distant, hollow rap of a hammer as a carpenter somewhere in the settlement plied his trade registering only slightly on his intent, grim-set consciousness. Securing the horse, and shifting the pistol on his hip to a more quickly accessible position, he crossed to the door in the back wall of the structure and entered.

He was in a narrow and dark hallway, saw that it led to the hotel's lobby at its opposite end. Moving along the corridor, spurs jingling softly, Jake made his way forward, halted when he reached the fairly large room filled with half a dozen chairs, a couple of tables, and a leather settee. Pictures hung on the walls, one of Abraham Lincoln, others of scenic nature, all in company with the mounted head of a large bear, its fangs bared menacingly as through dusty glass eyes it glared defiantly at those who viewed it.

Stepping farther into the room, Harper glanced about for the desk, located it beyond the stairway to his left. There was no one behind the short counter, and crossing to it, he tapped the call bell placed at one end.

At once a door beyond it opened, and a figure appeared. Jake drew up slowly. It was the woman who had been on the stagecoach with Yancey Richter and the drummer.

She recognized him in that same moment, and the half-smile of welcome on her lips froze, became a taut line.

"Yes?" she said coldly.

Harper nodded slightly. "This Henry Lavendar's place?"

The girl studied him with icy blue eyes. "It is. I'm Seera Lavendar."

She would have to be the outlaw's daughter, Jake realized. She was too young to be his wife, unless it was one of those spring-and-winter marriages.

"Call him."

Seera's lips trembled. "So you can kill him like you did that other man?"

"Between him and me," Harper replied in an emotionless voice. "Call him out here, or I'll go in there after him."

The girl looked down, and then, composure regained, she faced him, shook her head. "My father's dead, murdered. Whatever it is you want of him, you're too late."

Dead! Jake Harper's rigid shoulders came down slowly. Someone had beaten him to the outlaw, had cheated him out of collecting the law's due.

"When'd it happen?" he asked stiffly.

"Three weeks ago, more or less," Seera said grudgingly. "If you want to know anything more, I suggest you talk to Sheriff Dakin."

"About what I'll be doing," he murmured, the thought coming to him that Lavendar had been dead when he'd stopped the stage and had it out with Richter.

He was suddenly stalled, at a dead end. He had planned to have words with the outlaw first, pry information from him that would reveal the whereabouts of other gang members, and then settle up; instead he was facing the hostile daughter of Lavendar, from whom he could expect to learn nothing. But the setback was only temporary. The outlaw had lived in Oroville for some time, would have friends who could be of help.

Jake paused in his thinking as the screen door leading into the hotel from the street opened, slammed noisily. From the corner of an eye he saw the drummer who had been the girl's fellow passenger on the stagecoach enter, hesitate, and then approach slowly.

"Miss Lavendar . . . is there something wrong?" he wondered in a faltering voice.

Seera shook her head. "No. This man was asking for my father, that's all."

The drummer, frowning, considered Jake for several moments and then nodded. "You're the fellow back there on the road! Harper, I heard you say your name was. Hardly recognized you."

Jake made no comment. The drummer moved up to the counter, leaned against it.

"Henry Lavendar was shot—in the back," he volunteered. "The lady here's his daughter. She's taken over the hotel. Now, if there's anything I can do . . ."

"Doubt that."

"What I mean is, if there was something between you and her father, a business matter, I'll be glad to do what I can to settle—"

"Not what I came for," Harper cut in brusquely, and turned back to the girl. "Need a room. Expect to be around for a few days."

Seera Lavendar met his gaze coolly. "I don't rent rooms to outlaws—killers."

Anger flared through Harper. Outlaw! Killer! The impulse to tell the girl the truth, that it was her father who was the criminal and that the very property she now owned by inheritance came from money Henry Lavendar had killed to get, surged to his lips; but he resisted the urge. Seera could not be blamed for the sins of her father, and narrating them to her, while giving him satisfaction, would accomplish nothing except to further sadden and embarrass her.

It would be nice, however, Jake thought a bit ruefully, if she knew the truth, so that her low opinion of him could be altered.

"Happens you've got me figured wrong," he said, and bucked his head at the almost completely full key board on the wall behind her. "Appears to me you could use my business."

"The kind I can, and will, do without," the girl retorted. "As far as misjudging you, I saw what you did with my own eyes."

"I'll appreciate it, Mr. Harper, if you don't cause the lady any trouble," the drummer broke in, speaking carefully, almost pleadingly. "She's had a bad time of it, and I know that—"

"Forget it," Jake said gruffly, and pivoting on a heel, crossed the lobby to the hotel's entrance and stepped out onto the porch.

Seera watched Jake Harper stalk through the doorway and pause on the porch, his square-shouldered figure silhouetted against the sunlight of the street. Like Casey Kunkle, there'd been a moment or two during which she'd failed to recognize him—shaved, hair trimmed, and in new clothing—but one good look at his hard, determined features had brought back her memory.

As the indignation within her, aroused by his presence, subsided and her thinking became more rational, she wondered what it was that he wanted with her father. Evidently they had been acquainted, likely had business dealings of some sort, but to what extent her father could have involved himself with a man like Harper she could not even guess. Perhaps, if she hadn't allowed her feelings to get the best of her, she might have found out a few things about this Jake Harper as well as her father.

Actually, no one seemed to know Harper. When the stage had arrived in Oroville and the driver had called in the sheriff to view the body of Mr. Richter, the lawman said he did not know either the dead man or a gunman named Harper, qualifying the statement by adding that since he had lived in the settlement for only a year or so, that was not surprising. However, others in the crowd that had quickly gathered also disclaimed knowledge of . . .

"Miss Lavendar . . ."

Seera, jerked abruptly from her thoughts, glanced at the drummer questioningly.

"Just wanted to tell you—if that fellow Harper scares you any, I'll go to the sheriff, ask him to—"

"He doesn't frighten me," the girl replied, smiling.

She was being very careful when it came to Casey Kunkle. He'd been trying to warm up to her ever since they'd got to talking on the stagecoach, and it was necessary to hold him at arm's length. The increasingly warm attention he was showing her could only mean there was a proposal of marriage in the offing—one likely to come at the very moment she displayed even the smallest amount of encouragement. Casey Kunkle had said he entertained hopes of someday making his home in the west; evidently he had come to recognize in her his golden opportunity.

"Thought maybe him asking about your pa—father—"

"Some sort of business between them, I suppose," the girl said, eyes again on the tall figure standing on the porch. "Just what it might have been, I didn't bother to ask."

"Well, if he bothers you any, I'll talk to him about it."

Seera smiled, envisioning Casey Kunkle calling a man like Harper to account, but she masked her amusement with a hand, brushing it lightly across her lips, allowing her fingers to stray farther, straighten her hair.

"I doubt if it will be necessary," she said. "He seems a gentleman, despite the fact that he's ... well, a killer."

"Most times his kind are that way, sort of cool and polite, I mean. I know I couldn't do much with him, but he don't scare me none, either . . . and I could go to the sheriff, like I mentioned."

Seera smiled sweetly. "Thank you, Mr. Kunkle. I appreciate that, but I'll be all right. . . . Do you want your key?"

The drummer shook his head. "No, it just occurred to me while I was out there on the street that maybe you'd take supper with me tonight, and I came by to ask. They serve a fine meal at the Kansas Pride, and knowing you're still kind of tore up here . . ."

"That's very considerate of you, Mr. Kunkle," the girl said, "but I don't feel like going out just yet. I'm fixing my meals here in my own kitchen."

"Be pleased to keep you company here. . . ."

Seera forced another smile. Kunkle no doubt was a successful salesman if persistence was any criterion.

"Thank you, but I'd rather not. Perhaps some other time."

Nodding, she turned away, moved to the door that led into her living quarters. She heard Kunkle say something, but paid no heed, noting only as she entered the adjoining room that Jake Harper was still standing on the hotel's gallery.

~⤝ 10 ⤞~

Harper ran his gaze along Oroville's main street again, ticking off the signs on the store fronts as he sought to recognize a familiar name. All were strange to him.

He gave that thought. It was entirely possible that Henry Lavendar had been the only member of the gang to settle in Oroville, although there was no reason why the others should not. All had been cleared by the court, judged not guilty of any crime; thus there was no need to scatter and go into hiding.

That Richter had not chosen to live in the settlement was understandable. He had turned gambler, and as such, moved from town to town, stopping when he could find a high-stakes game, drifting on when the pickings grew thin or his luck turned sour.

Denver Bannock ... Matt Sandman ... Pete Garret. Jake once more reviewed the names on Oroville's business houses, seeking now to find one that in some way bore a resemblance or that would indicate a connection to any of the three remaining outlaws. He came up with nothing, but there were a few who had elected not to personalize their establishments, such as the owners of the Maricopa Saloon, the Kansas Pride

Restaurant, and the like; he'd make some inquiries, find out who their proprietors were.

With that in mind, he stepped off the gallery of the Cattleman's, and circling the building, returned to where he'd tied up the black. Freeing the leathers, he mounted, cut back to the street, and rode to the livery stable, scrutinizing closely every man he encountered along the way.

Turning into the low-roofed, shadow-filled structure, rank with smells of horse droppings and leather, Jake halted a short distance down the runway as a squat, thick-necked man emerged from a side room and approached him.

"Something I can do for you?"

Nodding, Harper came off the gelding. "Horse needs tending. Like to have him grained, watered, and rubbed down. Might take a look at his shoes. Could be wearing thin."

"You want him shod if they are?"

"Yeh, go ahead. . . . You Bill Williams?"

"Sure am," the livery-stable man answered, taking the black's reins. "When you aim to come back for him?"

"Tomorrow, maybe. Could be the next day."

Williams hawked, spat into the straw on the floor. "Glad to hear that. Damned hostler's off drunk again somewheres. I'm here alone."

"Way it goes sometimes. . . . Place around here where a man can get a room?"

"Cattleman's Hotel," Williams said promptly. "Just down the street a piece."

"Besides it."

The livery-stable owner eyed Harper critically. "You got something against hotels? It's a good, clean place, and the woman running it needs the business."

Somewhere back in the rear of the barn a horse set up a racket in his stall, kicking the thick plank sidings and lunging against his restraints.

"Damned stallion," Williams muttered when the commotion ceased. "Always acting up. . . . Was asking you—"

"Got my reasons," Jake said in a tone that ended the matter of the hotel. "Ought to be some other places."

"Well, there's the Maricopa Saloon, across the way. Can rent yourself a room there, but I ain't saying you'll get much sleep."

"Can try," Harper said, and started for the door. Midway he paused. "Fellow owning it, what's his name?"

"Jace Conway. Why?"

"Was thinking maybe a friend of mine was running it. Name's Bannock—Denver Bannock. Ever hear of him?"

Williams brushed at the sweat on his forehead with the back of his hand. "Nope."

"How about Pete Garret and Matt Sandman?"

"They supposed to live here?"

"Not sure. Sort of figured they did."

"Well, I been here more'n ten years, and I don't recollect any of them names. Must be some other town."

"Must've been," Harper said heavily, and continued on for the saloon.

Impatient with the way matters were going, Jake swore irritably. There should be some trace of Lavendar's partners in Oroville; it was only logical to believe they were there, or at some time in the past had been. Old friends, united by a crime in common from which they were later absolved, were bound to keep in contact; such was only human nature.

Stepping up onto the wide porch of the Maricopa, Harper crossed, moved through the open doorway, and slanted for the bar extending across the back wall of the building. It was a large saloon brightly lit and ornately furnished, and with a side room filled with tables, chairs, and gambling equipment. A balcony overlooked activities from the west side, and Jake could see the entrance to a hallway near its center. Whatever rooms were available would lie off it, he supposed.

Resting his elbows on the smooth, varnished counter, foot cocked on the brass rail, he nodded to one of the two bartenders on duty.

"Whiskey."

The aproned man slid a glass in front of him, filled it, and said, "Two bits."

Harper laid out the prescribed quarter, and taking up his drink, wheeled about and surveyed the room moodily. Two card games were in progress in the adjoining casino area, one with four players, the other with five, while a half-dozen bystanders and several saloon girls looked on. At the opposite end of the bar two cowhands conversed with a woman who had bright copper-colored hair.

Noting Jake's attention, she pulled away from the riders and sauntered toward him, a fixed smile on her rouged lips.

"Just passing through, stranger?"

Harper said, "More or less. Who do I see about getting a room?"

The redhead turned to the bartender who had served him. "Man's wanting a room, Zeke."

"This early in the day?"

"For tonight," Jake explained.

Zeke took a key from a box under the counter, dropped it before Jake. "Be two dollars. Take number two. It's the only one that's been cleaned up."

Harper dug into his cash, handed the barman the correct amount, and added two quarters.

"Fill me up again, and pour one for the lady."

Zeke obtained a second glass, complied with the order. Pocketing his key, Jake jerked his head at the scatter of empty tables and chairs in the casino.

"Any rule against us setting down in there, sister?"

"No, there ain't—and my name ain't sister, it's Letty," the redhead snapped, and led the way into the adjoining room.

Settling on a chair, she studied Harper quietly as he made himself comfortable. Then, "You got trouble, mister? You sure look like you just swallowed a mouthful of last month's leavings."

The humor was lost on Harper, still wrestling with the puzzle of where Henry Lavendar's partners could be, and the blank wall that the problem was throwing up in front of him. He shook his head, frowned; Letty just might know or have heard of the outlaws.

"Was expecting to find some jaspers here that I used to know," he said. "Haven't been able to locate them."

"You ask the sheriff? He's mighty strong on keeping track of everybody," the girl said, her tone scornful.

"No," Jake replied. "As soon not."

He was staying clear of the law for as long as possible, for questions on his part would lead to questions from the lawman, who would expect answers—and he had none he wished to give. Having Caleb Lynch somewhere in the offing, vowing to keep an eye on him, was bad enough.

Letty smiled knowingly, took a sip of her drink. She

had hard brown eyes, and there was a scar on the left side of her face that extended from the ear to her chin—a thin red line that she endeavored to cover with a generous application of rice powder, but failed.

"You and the tin stars ain't such good friends I see," she said. "Well, I'm on your side, mister, whoever you are."

"Name's Harper."

"Harper, eh," Letty said, and pausing, shifted her lackadaisical glance to the doorway. Three more riders were entering, shambling up on high-heeled boots and rattling spurs, to join the pair waiting at the bar.

"Bunch from the Hammond outfit," the woman said. "Ranch north of town. Long on drinking, and not much else."

The cowhands got together, laughing, jostling each other, swearing noisily as Zeke set out more glasses and began to fill them, skillfully spilling none of the liquor.

"Them jaybirds you're looking for—maybe I've come across them," Letty said, finishing off her drink. "Was you to stand me another round, I might do some thinking back."

Jake nodded. "Get us a bottle."

The woman rose, crossed to the bar, and returned immediately, paying no attention to a flurry of comments and observations from the cowhands. Refilling Harper's glass as well as her own, she rested her elbows on the table and considered him expectantly.

"Them friends—they got names?"

"Pete Garret," Jake said. "Little man with sandy hair and blue eyes. Good with his gun. . . . Denver Bannock. He's a bit on the heavy side, and he's got red hair. The last one's Matt Sandman. Tall, thin, eyes like a snake."

Letty's mouth pulled into a tight smile. "You spiel them descriptions off like you was John Law himself. You sure you ain't no—"

"I'm not," Harper cut in. "They sound familiar to you?"

The woman tossed off her drink, helped herself to another from the bottle. "Sure don't think they're anybody I've ever known, but that there last name—Sandman—it's sort of familiar."

"You remember it from around here or from somewhere else?"

"Ain't remembering if from no place, just that I think I've heard of him." Letty twisted about on her chair, faced the table where the five-handed card game was under way. "Marta!"

One of the girls leaning on the shoulder of a player looked around. "Yeh?"

"Come over here a minute."

Marta drew herself erect, wheeled, and started across the floor. Her high button shoes had red velvet inserts, Jake noticed, that matched the dress she was wearing.

"This here's Harper," Letty said, filling her glass and handing it to the woman. "He's hunting some friends. Name of one's Sandman. Didn't I hear you talking about somebody with that handle?"

Marta studied Jake suspiciously. "Maybe. What do you want with him?" she asked, sitting down.

"Like to find him," Harper said, "along with a couple others I know—Pete Garret and Denver Bannock."

"You ain't the law?"

"No, he ain't," Letty snapped, irritated. "You think I'd be setting here with him if he was? Expect the truth is that he's on the dodge—judging from the way he talks."

Marta nodded, satisfied. "I was working in Sandman's place before I come here—a saloon over in Junction City. Big, fancy layout—drinking, gambling, lots of girls."

Jake Harper had come to attention, but his cold, masklike features betrayed no more interest than could be expected of a man inquiring about a friend.

"Was sure he was around here somewhere.... What about the others?"

"Ain't never heard of a Pete Garret," Marta replied, helping herself to the whiskey, "but Bannock—I think a rancher that come into Sandman's ever' once in a while was called that. Ain't too sure. Could've been something that sounded like that."

Jake shrugged. "Well, knowing where Sandman is helps a lot. Can probably locate the others through him. This Junction City, it far from here?"

"About a day's ride," Letty said.

"More like a day and a half," Marta corrected.

Letty sniffed. "All depends on the horse, I reckon."

Marta's shoulders stirred indifferently. "You aiming to go see Matt?" she asked, rising and glancing toward the card players.

"Expect so."

"As soon you'd not tell him you been talking to me—we didn't exactly part friends," the girl said; and then added: "Never liked him much."

"Guess he hasn't changed any, then," Harper observed, and swung his eyes to the saloon's entrance.

A small, thin man with a full moustache and wearing a star pinned to his vest had come to a halt just within the doorway. He was elderly, and the hair peeping out from beneath his wide-brimmed hat was snow white. Arms folded across his chest, he surveyed the patrons in the room, paused when his gaze reached

Jake. Immediately then he resumed his slow, purpose-
ful stride.

"You got company coming, Harper," Letty said
dryly. "That there's the sheriff, Jess Dakin."

11

Jake eased back on his chair. He could thank the drummer he'd encountered at the Cattleman's Hotel for calling him to the lawman's attention, he supposed; or it could have been Seera Lavendar, still hoping to see him punished for cutting down Yancey Richter. No matter. A meeting was likely inevitable, anyway.

"Best you two move on," he said quietly. "Don't want you getting in bad with the law."

Marta was already sauntering off, returning to the poker players. Letty got to her feet, filled her glass, and began to follow.

"Good luck, Harper," she murmured.

Jake smiled briefly, nodded, his attention on the lawman coming to a halt a few steps from the table.

"Sit down," he invited.

The sheriff, jaw clamped tight, shook his head. "I'll do my talking standing. . . . Your name Harper?"

"Expect you know it is. Whoever told you I was here told you that, too."

"Can do without your lip," the lawman said icily. "I'm Dakin, the sheriff. Serving notice on you here and now to ride on. I don't want you around."

"You got a reason?"

"Plenty of them—main one being that killing you done. I don't put up with no shootouts."

"Wasn't in your town. Anyway, what's one tinhorn gambler less?"

"Makes no difference what he was to me. Killing is killing, and I won't stand for it."

Jake smiled coldly. "You didn't have to."

"But you hanging around here's going to mean another'n. I know your kind."

The saloon was in a deep hush, as everyone within its walls listened intently to the exchange of words. The cowhands from the Hammond ranch, at the end of the bar and therefore close to Dakin, began to pull back quietly, anticipating gunplay.

"Could be," Jake said, "but you can rest easy, sheriff. Nobody around here I aim to draw on. You've got my word on that."

"What the hell good's the word of somebody like you?" Dakin demanded angrily. "Now, I want you climbing on your horse and—"

Harper's voice was flat, and his eyes had taken on a brittle glint as he cut in sharply. "Forget it, Dakin. I know the law. You can't run me off unless you've got a reason—and you don't have one."

"Could be I won't need one," the lawman said slowly, quietly.

"Then I reckon it'll come down to one thing— whether you're big enough to do the job . . . or not."

The lines in Jess Dakin's face had tightened, and there was a bleakness to his manner. Jake felt a pang of regret. Being a lawman was a tough job, and he was wishing he hadn't backed the old man into a corner as he had, but it had come about almost without his realizing it—a normal reaction brought about by having been pushed around all those months by the guards in Big Lonesome, he supposed.

"I don't want any trouble with you, sheriff," he said, softening his tone. "There's no need for it. . . . And far as that shooting was concerned, it was a fair fight. I gave Richter a chance to draw; instead, he tried tricking me with a hideout gun. I got in the first bullet anyway. That drummer and the stagecoach driver—and the girl—saw it and can tell you that's how it was."

"Not saying it wasn't," Dakin said, seizing the opportunity to climb out of the hole he found himself in. "And whatever you had against him's your business— it's just that I won't have you coming into my town shooting up the place."

"No need for me to," Harper replied; and added: "Now."

One of the card players laughed. The sheriff's color darkened as his eyes narrowed.

"Fact is, I'll be riding on in the morning," Jake continued.

"All right," Dakin said briskly. "Reckon the morning'll do. Main thing is, I want you gone."

"Can depend on it."

"And something else—you're to stay inside here, and there ain't to be no trouble."

The Hammond cowhands were again stringing out along the bar, and the poker players, interest also waning, had returned to their game. The rapid drumming of a horse and rider passing by at full gallop along the street echoed in the big room, the sound at first only a faint tattoo that quickly rose to a loud hammering and then diminished gradually. Frowning, Dakin listened until the hoofbeats were no more, and then came back to Harper.

"I make myself clear?"

"Giving you my word."

The lawman shrugged. "For what it's worth. . . . You want to tell me what the trouble was between you and that gambler? Like to keep my records straight."

"Just set it down as something personal," Jake answered, definitely closing the subject with the chill in his tone.

"I see. I'll let it go at that. Now, I'm expecting you to be gone in the morning. . . ."

"I heard you, sheriff. Can do me a favor when you leave—drop by and tell Bill Williams that, so's he'll have my horse ready."

Dakin's color darkened again. "Run your own goddamn errands," he snapped, and pivoting, stalked rigidly out of the saloon.

Harper, reaching for his bottle, watched the lawman depart, again having a measure of regret for being so hard on the man, one such as he himself was once, and trying to do a job—but there was nothing to be done about it now; no one yet had figured out how to unspeak words that shouldn't have been given voice. Dissatisfied with himself, Jake glanced up as Letty came back to the table, a broad smile on her lips, empty glass in her hand.

"You sure cut him off at the whiskers!" she said admiringly. "Ain't never seen Dakin back down like that!"

"Man's getting old, I expect."

"He's been old ever since I've known him," the woman said, sinking onto a chair and pushing her glass toward him. "So you was the one that shot the gambler. Heard about it when the stage come hauling in his body. What was it all about? He crook you?"

"Reckon you could say that," Harper replied wryly as he poured the last of the whiskey into Letty's glass.

Caleb Lynch rode into Oroville shortly before dark, going immediately to Bill Williams' Livery Stable. Pulling up in the runway, he swung off his fagged horse and started down the row of stalls. At the third one he halted, a grunt of satisfaction coming from his lips. The black gelding standing slack-hipped inside the narrow box was Harper's. He'd found his man.

Turning, the lawman came face to face with an overall-wearing individual who had materialized quietly out of the stable's gloomy depths.

"Looking for somebody?"

"Found him," Lynch said. "Who're you?"

"Williams. This here's my place, and I want to know why you're sneaking—"

"You don't need to know nothing," Lynch broke in sharply, lifting the flap of his shirt pocket to display his star. "Where's the man who owns this black?"

"Over there," the stableman said, jerking a thumb at the Maricopa Saloon. "Was figuring to stay the night, I reckon, since he wanted to know about getting hisself a room, and then there was some kind of a ruckus he had with the sheriff, so he's—"

"Ruckus?"

"Yeh. Sheriff tried to run him out of town. Fellow same as told him to go to hell, said he'd leave when he got ready—in the morning."

Lynch had drawn up stiffly. "It end there—with no shooting?"

"Yep. Never come down to that, but them that was watching say it was mighty close. I missed it all, was shoeing this here horse of his at the time. Goddamn helper of mine, laying off drunk somewheres and leaving me to do—"

"Who's the sheriff here?"

"Name's Dakin, Jess Dakin. You after that fellow for killing the gambler, marshal?"

"What gambler?"

"Name of Richter, heard a drummer say."

Richter. . . . One of the outlaws that Harper had set out to find and execute. Damn it all to hell anyway! Why did he have to lose Jake Harper's trail and arrive too late to be on hand for the killing? It could have been the very incident that would give him grounds for throwing Harper back into the pen, or maybe even seeing him hang.

"How'd it happen?"

"This Harper took him off'n the stage, made him go for his gun. Gambler tried to outsmart him. Made out like he was backing down, then pulled a hideout pistol, one of them little nickel-plated forty-fours, the stage driver said. Harper still beat him to the trigger. Was a fair fight, and can't nobody fault him for being faster."

"No, reckon not," Lynch said, resentment stirring through him. He could expect Harper to manage it so's he'd be in the right; it was always that way during the time he was a lawman. Smart—and lucky, too.

"You know anybody around here by the name of Bannock or Sandman or Lavendar or Garret?" he asked then.

Williams dug into a pocket for a plug of black tobacco, bit off a corner. "Funny thing, Harper was asking about them, too—all except Lavendar."

"They live here?"

"Lavendar did. He's dead now. Them others—"

Caleb Lynch's seamy face hardened. "Harper kill Lavendar?"

"Not far as anybody knows. Happened about a month ago, and the sheriff's still trying to find out who done it. Lavendar run the hotel down the street a piece. Them others you mentioned, I ain't never heard of, 'cepting when Harper asked about them."

Lynch nodded absently. Jake Harper couldn't have been the one to gun down Henry Lavendar; he was still inside Higgtown prison a month ago. But he had caught up with Yancey Richter. Now there were only three of the gang left. If he could get a line on them, he just might be able to get to them ahead of Harper—and be there in time to pin something on him.

"Where'll I find the sheriff?"

Williams shifted his cud. "Most likely in his office," he said dryly. "Sort of where he hangs out."

"Jail was dark when I rode by."

The livery-stable owner shrugged. "Well, I sure don't know where he'll be, but there's one place where he won't—the Maricopa Saloon. That fellow Harper sure made a dang fool of him in there."

Too bad it didn't end up in a shooting, Lynch thought callously. Killing the town's lawman might have furnished the key he needed to put Jake Harper away for good. But he kept the idea to himself, only nodded to Williams.

"Look after my horse," he said. "I'll be back later."

⤙ 12 ⤚

Jake Harper became aware of a rider on his trail about noon that next day as he was topping a ridge on the road to Junction City. At first he thought it was just another pilgrim heading out of Oroville in the same direction as he, but when the rider matched the black's pace, neither drawing nearer when the gelding slowed nor falling behind when he quickened his gait, Jake knew he was being followed.

He'd gotten an early start, leaving the settlement well before first light in order to make Junction City by dark. He could easily do it, Bill Williams had assured him, and then had added that whoever had told him it would require a day and a half didn't know what he was talking about. The stableman had seemed a bit nervous during the conversation that took place while he was saddling the black, and Harper wondered now if the rider trailing him had anything to do with the man's fidgets.

Waiting until he had reached a rise in the road where a view of him would be cut off from whoever it was behind him, Jake rode into a stand of brush. Slouched in the saddle, he kept his eyes on the crown of the hump where the rider would first appear. He

had a strong hunch as to the identity of his pursuer—
Deputy Marshal Caleb Lynch—but he wanted to be
certain.

His belief proved to be correct. The lawman
crowned the ridge shortly, and began the long swing
down into the swale across which the roadway cut a
straight slash.

Lynch, not seeing his objective in the distance,
slowed his horse and began to look around, scanning
the nearby areas for sign. Failing, the lawman hurriedly put the buckskin he was riding to a fast gallop
for the opposite horizon.

Harper watched the lawman move off. Evidently the
marshal had been in the stable at the time he was making ready to leave, had warned Bill Williams to say
nothing of his presence. Hell, it didn't matter—let
Caleb Lynch follow. He had no need to fear the
federal lawman, since he had done nothing, and
planned nothing, that could be considered a crime.
But the marshal, hanging around making certain that
no law was broken, could become a nuisance.

Waiting until the lawman had dropped from sight
beyond the far rim of the swale, Jake set the black to a
lope, resuming a course that would take him to Junction City but avoiding the road and staying well within
the brush that paralleled it as much as possible.

If he guessed right again, Lynch would soon double
back, be looking for tracks leaving the highway.
Likely he did not know for certain that Junction City
was the destination of the man he was following, but
was only assuming such to be the fact.

Most likely he questioned Bill Williams and learned
that the settlement had been discussed. He would have
drawn a conclusion from that; but that's all it would
have been. Insofar as Letty and Marta, the two saloon

girls at the Maricopa, were concerned, Lynch would have gotten nothing from them. Their feelings toward lawmen had been only too evident.

Jake saw no more of the marshal after sidetracking him at the swale, and when he rode into the settlement around midafternoon, coming in from its east side, there was no sign of Lynch approaching along the established route to the north. Chances were good the man was still back somewhere in the area where he'd lost his quarry, searching for something, anything, that would give him a clue as to which direction the rider he followed had taken.

Junction City appeared to be about the same size as Oroville, and Matt Sandman's place, being the largest building along the street, was not difficult to locate. It was a broad, pitched-roof structure with a high, masking false front painted bright red. The name of its owner had been inscribed in bold black letters almost the full width of its facade, and beneath it in only slightly smaller size the words LIQUOR—GIRLS—GAMBLING—DANCING.

Pulling up to the hitchrack at the side, one that extended the length of the building and undoubtedly was capable of standing no less than fifty horses, Harper dismounted, secured the black, sweaty from the long, steady journey, and entered the saloon.

As Marta had said, Sandman's place was on a grand scale. It had a lengthy bar behind which mirrors glittered from the mellow lamplight cast by a dozen or so circular chandeliers; a complete casino, where a patron could buck the tiger in the game of his choice; a fairly large raised platform upon which a man could indulge himself in dancing with one of the numerous brightly clad girls to the accompaniment of a piano stationed at its far end.

Jake let his eyes run the wide room, the ceiling of which was supported at strategic points by square wooden pillars variously adorned with pictures, deer antlers, and Indian arrows gathered to a common center with rawhide strips to form a design. The furnishings looked expensive—dark wood tables and chairs, the mahogany counter with its shining brass, and of course the well-stocked shelves beyond it laden with bottles and glassware.

Matt Sandman had done right well with his portion of the bloodstained gold, too, Harper thought, as, grim-set, he crossed to the bar, where four bartenders were on duty. All but one of the crew were lounging at the rear of the generous area back of the counter, evidently awaiting the night's rush that was yet to come.

Ordering a drink from the aproned man seeing to the needs of the two dozen or so customers presently in the saloon, Harper paid when his order was promptly filled, and taking up the glass, wheeled, hooked his elbows on the edge of the bar, and looked out over the room in search of Sandman.

He did not see the outlaw among the patrons and dealers, and waving away one of the girls who moved toward him, he tossed off his drink, came back around, and setting the glass on the counter, fixed his cold glance on the bartender.

"Where'll I find Sandman?"

At the question, the aproned man jerked a thumb at a door in the rear of the saloon. "In his office, I reckon, but he's busy."

Ignoring the words, Jake moved off along the counter for Sandman's business quarters.

"Said he was busy," the bartender said, raising his voice.

Harper did not slow his step, but continued on. He

heard the barkeep call out again, this time to a thick-shouldered man slouching in a chair at the end of the counter.

"Got a smart one, Lat. Get rid of him," he said.

Cool, Jake watched the big man, one of Sandman's bouncers, he assumed, rise to his feet and take up a position in front of the entrance to the outlaw's office.

"Back up, friend," Lat warned. "Like Earl said, the boss's busy."

Harper did not break stride. The bouncer's shoulders came up, and his head thrust forward belligerently.

"You hard of hearing or something?"

"Get out of my way," Harper said quietly.

Lat's hamlike fists doubled into clubs. "Ain't telling you again. Move on. Matt's busy."

"He'll see me," Jake replied, and taking a long, sudden step forward, drove a left into the man's belly.

Breath exploded from Lat's flared mouth as he buckled. Harper's right arm came up. Lamplight glinted off the pistol in his hand as it struck, with a solid thud, against the bouncer's head. The big man dropped solidly to the floor.

It had all been done efficiently, quickly, and hardly anyone but the bartenders and two or three patrons standing nearby were aware of what had taken place.

Holstering his weapon, Jake Harper threw a warning look at the men behind the counter, and stepping over Lat's prostrate figure, he opened the office door and stepped inside.

The shadow-filled room, furnished with a table, a half-dozen chairs, and a leather couch, was empty. Closing the panel behind him, Harper crossed to a window in the wall opposite and raised the thick green shade, allowing sunlight to flood the room.

Wheeling, he drew up short, glance falling to the body of a man lying face-down beside the table. A pearl-handled knife—a stiletto—was in his back. Jake knelt, and grasping the figure by the hair, looked closely at the chalky face. It was Matt Sandman.

⤙ 13 ⤚

Harper, swearing softly, drew himself erect. Someone had beaten him to another of the outlaws; it was as if some mysterious person was moving ahead of him, searching out and putting an end to the men he'd vowed to kill before he could act.

That such could be a fact was out of the question, he knew. No one was deliberately cheating him of his intentions; it was just luck that so far was playing a very large part in the affair—his accidental encounter with Yancey Richter, the murder of Henry Lavendar by some person unknown, and now this.

Harper shrugged, brushed aside the impatience that he felt. The outlaw was dead, and whoever it was that had plunged the thin, double-edged knife into his back deserved a vote of thanks for ridding the world of a cold-blooded killer. He should be glad the job had been done for him, Jake realized.

He heard the catch in the door lock click, turned as the panel swung open. A dark-skinned, full-bodied woman, her red and blue spangled dress cut low at the neck to display a swelling bosom, stepped inside. She had large black eyes, a wealth of glossy hair, also black, and for several moments she paused, as if transfixed, staring at Harper, with the door only partly closed behind her. And then, as she saw the body of Matt Sandman on the floor, a shrill scream broke from her lips.

"Matt's been murdered!" she cried, whirling about to face the saloon. "Man that done it's still in here!"

Beyond the woman, Jake heard shouts, the sudden scrape of chairs on the floor, the hammer of boot heels as everyone in the building surged toward the girl. Stepping back, he waited, eyes on the now open doorway.

"Come out of there, Cameo," a deep voice commanded, and as the girl disappeared into the crowd gathering at the room's entrance, Earl, the bartender, followed by Lat and several men, pushed into the outlaw's office. Harper, gun out of its holster and in his hand, met them in cold silence.

"Used a knife," Earl said, glancing at Matt Sandman's body. "Reason we never heard no shot." He swung his attention to Jake. "Might as well drop that pistol and give up, mister. You won't be getting past all of us."

"Wasn't me that killed him," Harper said. "He was laying there dead when I came in."

One of the men laughed. "We just knowed you'd be saying that, but you ain't squirming out of it. We got you dead to rights."

"Should've figured that's what you was aiming to do—busting in here like you done," a second voice added.

Jake ignored the comments, glanced at Lat. There was a large discoloration on the side of the man's face where he'd taken the blow from the pistol, and his eyes were bright with anger.

"Who was in here before me?" Harper asked. "Being right outside like you were, you'll know."

Sullen, the bouncer shook his head. "You was the only one that went in to see Matt."

"All day?"

"Hell no, not all day! Been a lot of going and coming. The girls, Earl, couple of ranchers. Me, too, once or twice. But he was still living while that was going on. Talked to him myself no more'n a hour ago."

"It's the last thirty minutes I'm asking you about."

"You was the only one going in," Lat said doggedly. "Reckon I ought to know, being here and—"

"We're just wasting time," Earl, the bartender, broke in. "Did somebody go after the marshal?"

"Ernie King did," a man in the crowd replied. "Ought to be getting here pretty quick."

Harper's jaw tightened. Convincing Matt Sandman's friends that he had nothing to do with the murder would be an impossibility, and getting thrown into a cell was something he had no time for. Like as not the real killer would be found, since the weapon used was far from common, and inquiry and investigation were certain to turn up its owner, but he was not about to sweat it out in a cage while such search was being conducted, if indeed one was.

And there was every likelihood that it would not be deemed necessary. Lat, the bartenders, the saloon girl, Cameo, and seemingly everyone else in the building were certain he was the killer and would testify against him.

Jake glanced at the window in the wall behind him. The sash was partly raised, offered an exit. Edging toward it, he faced Lat and the half-dozen others who had ventured into the room and now stood crowded in the doorway awaiting the arrival of the town marshal.

"Stay put," he warned in a hard voice. "I'm going out this window. First man that makes a move to stop me's dead."

"Running, eh?" Earl said scornfully. "Thought you claimed you didn't kill him."

"Wasn't me, but you've already got your minds made up, and I'm not about to hang for what somebody else done."

"Let's rush him," a man beside Earl suggested. "He sure can't shoot us all."

The bartender gave that brief thought, shrugged. "I ain't that anxious to die. Besides, he won't get far."

Harper wedged a finger under the hook in the window, raised it to the top. Forty-five in his free hand and leveled at the motionless crowd, he thrust a leg through the opening and backed out.

"Earl's giving you good advice," he said quietly as he felt solid ground under both feet. "Not in my mind to hurt anybody, but if it comes down to any of you trying to stop me, I will. . . . Tell your marshal to look for whoever owns that fancy knife. He finds out, then he's got the killer."

A quick rumble of voices followed Harper's words, none of what was said being intelligible to him as he spun on a heel and hurried toward the side of the saloon where he'd tied his horse. Rounding the corner of the building, he saw the gelding standing patiently at the rack with several other mounts, and rushed on.

There was no one in sight along the street as he stepped up onto the saddle; he guessed about everybody had gathered inside the saloon, but that would not hold true for long. They'd be after him in only moments; but moments were all he needed, he thought grimly, to get out of the town and lose himself in the hills.

Bannock. . . . Denver Bannock. He realized suddenly that he hadn't asked about the outlaw. Marta
had said she thought he was a rancher and that he
lived somewhere around Junction City. He'd not get a
chance to return to the settlement and make inquiries
regarding the man; best he stretch his luck and take
time now.

Spurring the black into the street, he rode hard for
its lower end. Shouts were coming from the alley behind Matt Sandman's saloon, and he reckoned some of
the bolder onlookers had taken it upon themselves to
start the pursuit.

But there was no one along the sidewalks as the
black raced toward the last of the buildings in the double row, and when he pulled off to the side of a small
ragtag saloon set back from the other buildings at the
edge of the settlement, it occurred to him that he possibly would find no one available to ask directions of if
all of the town's residents were at the scene of the excitement.

Entering the saloon, lit only by a pair of wall lamps,
Jake glanced around. A woman was standing in a
doorway behind the crude bar, a broom in her hand.
She was apparently the wife of the owner. Harper
touched the brim of his hat with a forefinger.

"Looking for the Bannock place—ranch somewheres close to here. You tell me how to get there?"

The woman nodded. "Reckon I can. . . . What's all
the hullabaloo down the way? The mister went tearing
out of here like his britches was on fire."

"Matt Sandman's been killed. The Bannock ranch.
Where—"

"Sandman's dead, eh? Well, good riddance. . . .
Bannock's? It's west of here, about ten miles—right
next to the mountain. . . . They know who killed him?"

"Not for sure," Harper said, turning for the door. "Obliged to you for the help."

The woman made a reply, but Jake was already out of the narrow dark building and trotting toward his horse. The shouting near Sandman's place had increased, and it came to him that he'd be fortunate to get out of the town before the posse that undoubtedly was being organized caught sight of him.

If they did and immediately gave chase, he would need to throw them off, since Bannock's place lay only a short distance away, and they would be on him before he could reach the outlaw's ranch and settle with him. Best he head south out of the settlement until he could shake the posse, and then double back. They would have no idea of his intentions.

Cutting the black about, Harper dropped back to the street and rode into the open, the only course open to him, as a wire fence strung across the yard behind the saloon prevented his continuing on through. Instantly a yell went up from the crowd gathered in front of Sandman's.

"There he is!" someone shouted.

"Get to the horses!" a second voice cried.

Jake Harper grinned tightly, and raking the black with his spurs, headed him for the brushy hills to the south.

Caleb Lynch shrugged wryly as Junction City came into sight. Twice Jake Harper had thrown him off the trail, once right at the start, although he really couldn't blame that on the onetime lawman, and again there on the road out of Oroville; and it just could be he was now heading into a blind alley.

After Harper had given him the slip in that big swale, he'd doubled back, thinking to find the tracks left by the black horse the ex-convict was riding and resume his place behind him. He'd failed—thanks to that goddamn Indian turn of mind that Harper had—for there was no trace of the man.

Lynch had mulled that about in his head for a while, and then, abandoning any hope of locating tracks, he'd continued on for Junction City. There was no guarantee that Harper was going there, but it seemed likely. For one thing, it was the only town of any size in that part of the territory, and for another, Harper had asked Bill Williams, the livery-stable owner in Oroville, about it. That, of course, could have just been a blind and Harper's way of throwing off anyone trailing him.

Turning into the street at the end of the settlement, the lawman drew to a halt, eyes on the high red-painted front of the town's largest building. SANDMAN'S, the lettering read. Matt Sandman. . . . Another of the outlaws Jake Harper maintained had been involved in the murder of Josh Moon and his wife. The lawman grunted in satisfaction. There was no longer any doubt that Junction City had been Harper's destination.

Somewhere along the way, possibly in Oroville, Harper had learned of Sandman's whereabouts, and after discovering the leader of the gang dead by someone else's hand, and with Yancey Richter's scalp under his belt, he'd set out at once to add another notch to his gun—all in the name of justice.

The marshal swore. Harper was there ahead of him, probably had already sought out Sandman and gunned him down. That the outlaw might have killed Harper did not occur to him, mostly because the possibility of anyone matching Jake Harper's skill with a sixgun was very remote.

There was nothing to do but ride on in, have a talk

with the local lawman, and see what had . . . Caleb Lynch closed down on his thinking, centered his attention on the front of Sandman's. Men were pouring out of the doorway into the open, coming around from the side of the building, shouting back and forth.

Something had already happened, he realized, and that something could only be Jake Harper finishing up the job he insisted the law had failed to do. A posse was being mounted, he saw then; men were leading up horses.

At that moment, at the opposite end of the street, a rider on a black horse spurted into view. Harper! There was no mistaking him. Yells went up again from the crowd in front of the saloon, and men started swinging onto their saddles, but Harper was well under way.

Lynch dug his spurs into the buckskin he was riding, broke the horse into a run. He reckoned he'd best get down there in a hurry, learn the details of what had happened. This just could be the time he was hoping for—the one where that son-of-a-bitch Jake Harper had slipped up and bought himself a hanging!

⭐ 14 ⭐

The low hills, with their forests of dense brush and glistening black rocks, were just ahead. Jake Harper flung a glance over his shoulder. The Junction City posse, a dozen strong, was strung out behind him and coming on fast.

He brushed at his jaw, bent lower as he returned his attention to the ragged country he was entering. He hadn't figured on the party moving out so quickly, but he reckoned he still had enough of a lead to shake them.

Cutting off the road, Harper dropped into a narrow wash. Following it for a short distance to where it merged with a wide and fairly deep arroyo, he again veered the gelding, held him to a good lope along the sandy floor of the gash for a quarter-mile or so, and then swung up and out of it into a cluster of cedars.

The black was wheezing for wind, his sides pumping wildly; halting deep within the scrubby trees, Harper settled back to wait. Moments later he heard the drumming of the posse as it swept by on the road. Jake grinned, patted the gelding's wet neck. The riders had missed the point where he'd turned off into the gully. It was an error, however, that they would dis-

98

cover quickly, since the road, stretching out before them for miles, was in the open and afforded good visibility, and his disappearance would be immediately noted.

Best he get out of the area as fast as possible. Roweling the black, Jake returned to the arroyo and doubled back over the tracks the gelding had just made, leaving a confused trail of overlying and intermingling hoof prints. He maintained that procedure until he reached the narrow wash where he had forsaken the road, and there he climbed up to where he was once more on high ground.

On a level with the road, and in a thicket of mixed brush, Harper halted, listened for sounds of the posse, possibly already aware of their mistake and doubling back. But he could hear nothing but the far-off mourning of a dove and concluded he was still in the clear.

Bringing the gelding about, still careful to keep the big horse walking on his own trail, Harper rejoined the road. There he continued north, in the direction of the settlement, until a gravelly shoulder offered an exit that would not record the black's passage, and swung onto it.

He pulled up instantly, anger coursing through him. Just beyond a stand of shoulder-high rabbitbush, Marshal Caleb Lynch faced him, a leveled pistol in his hand.

"Figured you'd be coming back by here," the lawman said with a humorless smile. "Climb down."

For a long breath Jake Harper did not move, and then, slowly, he came off the saddle. Inwardly he was cursing himself for his carelessness and for dismissing the lawman from his mind. He knew Lynch was trailing him, keeping a close watch, hoping he'd make a mistake; he shouldn't have written the man off back there on the Oroville–Junction City road. But what did Lynch know that gave him reason to step in now? Had it to do with Sandman's death?

"Just knew you'd pull some kind of a stunt like this on that posse," the lawman said, nodding in satisfaction. "Reason I hung back, let them ride on when I spotted your tracks heading off into that wash."

"So?" Harper murmured, feeling his way.

"So I got you right where I want you, Harper, dead cold with a murder on your hands. . . . Just don't get no notions about that gun you're wearing—"

"What murder?" Jake broke in, eyeing Lynch narrowly. "If you're talking about Yancey Richter . . ."

"I ain't. That was a fair fight, so I been told, which don't mean nothing. You pushed Richter into it, knowing all along you'd outdraw him."

"Had nothing to do with Henry Lavendar's killing, either."

"Know that, too."

"Then who—"

"Don't act dumb with me, Harper! You know I'm talking about Matt Sandman. That's why that posse's chasing you—for killing him. You stubbed your toe there, mister, and I aim to see you swing for it."

"Wasn't me that stuck that knife in him," Jake said quietly. "He was dead when I walked into his office."

"Not the way them witnesses are telling it. They say he was all right until you bulled your way in to see him."

"What witnesses?" Harper asked, beginning to cast about for a means to escape.

"You know what witnesses!" the marshal snapped. "Them bartenders, that bouncer he kept hanging around, and his woman—along with a dozen of them that was in the saloon at the time. . . . Now, I want you to reach across yourself and pull that gun you're wearing, and let it drop. Then you'll unbuckle your belt and let it drop."

"They're lying," Harper said. "They just think he was alive when I went in that room, but he sure as hell wasn't. . . . You want to arrest somebody for his murder, then look up that woman—Cameo, I think they call her. Acted to me like she knew he was dead when she showed up."

"Wouldn't be her. They tell me Sandman and her was going to marry. Ain't likely she'd kill him."

Harper shrugged, still making no move toward his weapon. "You're working mighty hard to get something on me, marshal."

"I've *got* something on you," the lawman replied decisively. "And it's going to hang you."

"Why're you taking it on yourself, special like, to nail me?"

"Because it ain't right you running loose like you are and doing what you're aiming to do. That damn judge was wrong in getting you pardoned, and it's up to me to change it. . . . You dropping that gun? I'd as soon put a bullet in your head as not—and I'd be within my rights, because I'm apprehending a killer."

Harper glanced to the south. The posse would be returning soon, and if he stalled long enough, their coming back onto the scene undoubtedly would put a crimp in the plans Caleb Lynch had for him. But he would be no better off; he'd still end up in the Junction City jail unable either to prove himself innocent of Matt Sandman's murder or to continue on his way to settle with Denver Bannock and the last of the outlaws, Pete Garret, wherever he might be.

"Where was you headed?" Lynch asked suddenly, as if remembering. "Sure wasn't going back to town."

"Maybe," Jake said. Evidently the lawman didn't know about Bannock and that he lived on a ranch nearby. "I've got to prove it wasn't me that put a knife in Sandman's back. Place to do that's right where it happened, and I've got to do it myself. Law's sure not going to help."

"Law don't need to do nothing," Lynch said coldly. "Whole thing's clear as daylight. . . . I'm saying it only once more, Harper. Get rid of that gun you're wearing. And I'm just hoping you try tricking me so's I can unload my forty-five into your guts!"

Jake smiled wryly. "You're a real credit to that badge of yours, Lynch. Government ought to be right proud of you."

The lawman nodded. "I'm feeling the same toward you as you do toward the Lavendar bunch."

"Meaning you think they're guilty and oughtn't to've gone free?" Harper said, again glancing down the road. Time was slipping away. If he was to make a break for it, it should be within the next few minutes. The posse would be drawing near.

"Means I ain't got no use for you. Never have, never will. Far as them others are concerned, I don't give a goddamn about them. It's you I set my cap for, and I got you. With the witnesses I'll have, you'll hang for sure, and—"

"Can't figure out where you got all that hate, marshal," Harper said, studying the weapon in the lawman's hand. The pistol was cocked, ready to go off at the slightest pressure of Lynch's trigger finger. "What did I ever do to you?"

"Maybe nothing to me—it's just that high-and-mighty way of yours," Lynch blurted, and caught himself.

Jake's shoulders stirred. He slid another quick look

to the road, said, "Never meant to tromp on your corns. Was always just trying to do my job."

"That gun," Lynch said in an icy tone. "You better be dropping it. And don't keep hoping that posse'll show up. You're my prisoner, and I'm taking you straight back to Big Lonesome for safekeeping while I get things set up."

Harper sighed, reached for his pistol with his left hand, lifted it from the holster, and allowed it to fall to the ground.

"The belt . . ."

Jake released the buckle of the cartridge-filled band of leather, let it drop alongside the gun.

"Now, step back."

Jake shrugged, drew away from the weapon. Lynch bucked his head in approval, and moving forward, bent down to retrieve the weapon, holstering his own as he did. In that brief space of time Jake Harper, realizing that such likely would be his only opportunity for escape, reacted.

He kicked out, drove the sharp toe of his boot into Caleb Lynch's belly. The lawman staggered back, tried to bring the pistol he'd picked up by the barrel into play. Harper was on him in a lunging leap. His big hand wrapped about the lawman's wrist, and bringing it down hard against his own knee, he knocked the gun loose as they both went sprawling to the ground.

"Goddamn you—jumping me! I'll—"

Harper had no time for words. As they struck the rocky, sun-baked soil, he grabbed at the marshal's pistol, jerked it clear of the leather, and rolling away, bounded upright. Dropping back a step, he recovered his own weapon, and then, breathing hard, a pistol in each hand, he watched Caleb Lynch struggle to his feet.

"Turn around," Harper ordered when the older man had regained his stance.

Lynch glared. "Reminding you of something! I'm a federal officer, and you're—"

"Seems you're the one that needs to be remembering that," Jake said coldly.

When the lawman had turned his back completely, Harper crossed to the buckskin the man was riding, and digging into the saddlebags, found the pair of chain-linked handcuffs that were standard equipment for such lawmen. Returning to where Lynch stood, he drew the marshal's arms back, affixed the manacles to his wrists.

"On your horse!"

Lynch turned woodenly, moved to the buckskin, halted. "How the hell you expecting me to climb up with my hands behind me?" he demanded angrily.

For reply Harper caught the slightly built man under the arms and boosted him onto the saddle. Then, unloading the pistol he'd taken from him, Jake dropped the empty weapon into the pouch where he'd found the handcuffs and buckled the straps.

"Where you taking me?" Lynch asked in a tight voice. His eyes had narrowed from suspicion, and sweat stood out on his leathery face in patches. "Off in some gully where you can put a bullet in my back?"

Harper, hooking the buckskin's reins over the saddlehorn, and making them secure, once more threw a glance to the road. The posse was still not in sight.

"Not taking you anywhere, marshal. You're going to town."

There was a long moment of silence, and then Lynch began to swear wildly as he envisaged himself riding into Junction City, helpless, arms pinned behind his back with his own manacles, empty pistol in his saddlebags.

"By God, Harper, you do this to me and I'll—"

"Brought it on yourself," Jake cut in quietly. "If you'd minded your business and forgot about trying to get back at me, it wouldn't've happened."

"Hunting down outlaws—that is my business!"

"But I'm no outlaw, marshal; you're forgetting that. And if you're riding my back because I've been in the pen, then you're wrong again. I served my time."

"Not all of it!" Lynch fairly shouted.

"Long enough to satisfy them, I guess. It was the governor that signed the pardon, not me," Harper said, leading the buckskin onto the road and pointing him for the settlement.

"I'm warning you!" Lynch yelled. "You better not do this to me, 'cause I'll sure hunt you down and—"

"So long, Caleb," Jake said indifferently, and stepping to the rear of the buckskin, slapped the horse smartly on the rump and sent him trotting off up the road.

Weaving uncertainly on the saddle, the lawman cursed again, voiced more threats, but Jake Harper was turning away, glancing at the sun, his thoughts on other problems.

It wouldn't be too long until dark, and he had to find Denver Bannock and settle with him before then, otherwise he'd likely have not only the posse to worry about, but very possibly the old marshal would again be on his trail.

~ 15 ~

Two towering pine-tree poles, adzed to smoothness and across the tops of which a squared timber had been placed, supported a hanging plank sign bearing Denver Bannock's name.

Jake Harper rode in under it, and staying on the well-marked road, guided the black toward a cluster of structures nestled in a grove a quarter-mile in the distance. Reaching the clearing where they sat, barren except for clumps of small desert daisies and scrub grass, he pulled up to the hitchrack in front of the flat-roofed main house and halted.

On beyond it he had noticed the corrals, the bunkhouse, barn, various sheds, and the cook shack, from which was coming the clatter of plates and other utensils. It was just about sundown, and Bannock's crew had gathered for the evening meal.

Harper gave that thought as he swung off the saddle. If Bannock ate with his hired hands, a confrontation would be more difficult—not that it posed any great personal problem, but he felt it best to have it out with the outlaw where there would be no interference; being forced to turn on and gun down a man, or men, who were only just innocent bystanders and who out of loyalty believed they should take a hand, was something he wished to avoid.

Tying the gelding to the rack, Jake crossed to the porch, no more than a landing that jutted out from the doorway, and knocked.

At once he heard the drag of chair legs as someone pushed back from a table. Satisfaction filled him. Bannock evidently took his meals in the main house, and it could even be that the outlaw was married, had children. If true, it was to be regretted, for it changed nothing insofar as Jake Harper and his purpose were concerned; the innocent suffering because of the guilty was a fact as old as time itself.

Arms folded across his chest, hat pushed to the back of his head, all else but a cold contemplation of the moments that lay ahead wiped from his mind, Harper waited. Somewhere out near the corrals a jackass brayed raucously, and in a piñon tree off the corner of the house a camprobber flitted about in the close confinement of gnarled limbs, scolding noisily.

The door swung back. Jake tensed as a squat individual wearing a leather vest and checked shirt, gun low on his hip, stood framed in the opening. Harper's rigid shape eased. It wasn't the outlaw.

"What d'you want?" the heavy-faced man demanded in a surly tone, and then, before Jake could speak, added, "We ain't hiring, if you're looking for work."

"Want to see Bannock," Harper replied coolly.

"Who're you?"

"Don't see as that matters to you. Get Bannock."

The husky man bristled. "The hell you say! I'm ramrodding this outfit, and the boss told me—"

"Who is it, Lige?" a deep voice called from the interior of the house.

"He ain't said. Wanting to see you."

Again there was the sound of a chair being moved. Harper took a step forward, started through the doorway. Lige, features angry, hurried to block his way.

Harper shouldered the man roughly aside. Cursing, Lige reached for the gun at his hip. Jake drew fast, his movements little more than a blur. His arm came up, hand gripping his own weapon, and all in one smooth swing clubbed the foreman solidly across the head. Lige groaned, sank to his knees.

"Stay out of this," Harper snarled, and turned his attention to an inner door, where motion caught his eye.

It was Denver Bannock. The outlaw, older-looking, his red hair thinner, pale eyes bright, was facing him uncertainly, a frown knitting his brow.

"Remember me?" Harper asked softly, holstering his forty-five.

For answer Bannock jerked back into the room, slammed the intervening door. Jake heard the lock click as he lunged toward it, halted when he came up against the thick closed panel. On beyond it he heard the rapid beat of boot heels and the slam of another door. It could mean only one thing: the outlaw was making an escape out the back of the house, where he could mount one of the horses waiting for its rider at the corral and flee into the wooded, brushy hills just west of the ranch.

A hard, grim smile on his lips, Harper pivoted, came about squarely against Lige, now on his feet and closing in on him. He ducked the wild swing the foreman aimed at his jaw, drove his left deep into the man's belly. Lige gasped, staggered forward. Impatient, Harper again drew his gun, rapped the man once more sharply over the ear, drove him to the floor.

Hurrying, Jake moved on for the door, but the blow

had only stunned the foreman. He felt Lige's arms wrap about his legs, fought to maintain balance, failed, and went down. Cursing at being delayed, Harper brought his weapon into play for the third time, laying the barrel across the bridge of the squat man's nose. Lige howled, released his grip, and Jake lunged to his feet.

"Damn you to hell!" the foreman shouted, and ignoring the blood streaming down his face, clawed out his pistol.

Harper stepped in closer, kicked the weapon from the man's hand, sent it skittering across the bare floor and out onto the landing.

"Stay where you are!" Jake snapped. "Get in my way again and I'll kill you!"

Moving past the prone Lige, he rushed into the open, pausing only to pick up the foreman's weapon and hurl it off into the weeds. In that same moment he caught the quick beat of a horse racing away from the rear of the ranch buildings, and breaking into a run, he crossed the yard to the black, yanked the leathers free, and vaulted onto the saddle.

Cutting the gelding about, he swung to the left of the house, thus avoiding the hardpack behind it, which he knew by then would be filled with curious hired hands wondering what all the excitement might be.

"Stop him, somebody!"

Lige's strident voice brought Harper half-around as the black pounded toward the corner of the building. A rifle blasted, and Jake, crouching low, whipped out his pistol. The foreman had obtained the weapon from a rack in the room apparently, was trying to bring him down, had luckily missed.

Jake Harper gave the man no second chance. He steadied briefly, snapped a shot at Lige, saw the man recoil against the door frame as the bullet drove into him. The rifle fell from his fingers as he reached for his left shoulder and slowly settled onto the landing.

Harper raked the black with his spurs, sent him racing on, rounding the corner of the house and driving hard for the first outcrop of trees, into which Denver Bannock, on a dark-colored horse, was disappearing some five hundred yards away.

Abruptly two men spurted into the open from between the cook shack and a wagon shed. Pistols drawn and leveled, they were obeying Lige's shout.

Harper drove them both back with a shot that sprayed dirt over their feet before they could act. Yells were now coming from the yard, and as the gelding thundered by the two men scurrying for shelter behind the cook's quarters, Jake could see Bannock's hired hands running toward the corrals, where horses would be waiting. If the mounts had yet to be saddled and bridled, he would have a few more minutes' start on them; if not, he could expect a half-dozen or more Bannock riders on his trail immediately.

Such would likely be the way of it, he thought as the black galloped across an open flat for the jutting wedge of brush and trees into which Bannock had vanished; the outlaw had ridden off shortly after he'd run from the house—proof that there had been a horse standing and ready to go.

Harper reached the trees and the foot of the slope along which they grew at the moment a small group of Bannock's cowhands came streaming out from the opening near the wagon shed. A taut grin pulled at his lips. It was going to be a tight one—his getting to Bannock before the outlaw's men could overtake him. But he'd make it, and while he had no illusions as to his chances against a half-dozen or more riders all bent on gunning him down, he'd manage somehow to collect the law's due from Denver Bannock before they got him.

✐ 16 ✐

Wheeling into the fringe of trees, Harper recoiled as two quick shots from Bannock's gun greeted him. Cursing, he cut the black about sharply. The outlaw had been waiting for him; he should have expected it.

Crouched low on the saddle, he veered the gelding in behind a mound covered with rock and tangled mountain mahogany. Circling to his right, he bore straight into a pocket of junipers and scrub oak that offered a dense screen, stopped. Eyes straining, he endeavored to locate the outlaw—somewhere above him on the tree-studded slope, and not too far, if he was to judge from the shots.

"Spread out . . . spread out!" a voice yelled from the foot of the hill.

Harper swore again. Bannock's riders had reached the edge of the flat, were entering the brush. They were below him, and immediately Jake spurred away, wanting to take advantage of the space that separated him from them as much as possible.

He could hear the rattling of loose gravel and the crackling of brush, and using that as a marker, rode the black farther right, climbing the slope at a long

112

tangent, all the while searching the shadowy hillside both above and to his left for Bannock.

He saw the outlaw minutes later. Bannock, riding a spotted gray, was moving slowly toward a rocky bluff on the crown of the slope. The man was proceeding quietly, carefully, evidently unaware of his pursuer's whereabouts and taking every precaution not to attract attention to his position.

Harper had expected the outlaw to immediately turn about upon the arrival of his hired hands and join them, believing safety would lie in numbers, but either it hadn't occurred to him or else he thought danger lay somewhere in between, and he was of no mind to risk the change.

Jake twisted about, threw his glance down the cluttered slope in an effort to locate Bannock's riders. At first he saw no one, and then, motion farther below caught his attention, and he had a fleeting view of a man and horse as they crossed an aisle between the pines. The men were much lower than he'd figured them to be, and seemingly were working toward the south. With night beginning to rise, they soon would find it difficult to see.

Harper nodded in grim satisfaction. Bannock was heading into high country. Daylight would hold there for some time after it was gone from the lower levels, since darkness started at the floor of the valleys and arroyos and gradually crept upward to the ridges and high bluffs rather than settled over the land. The bald, ragged peaks of the mountains were always the last to feel the warm touch of the sun's light.

Bannock, in his frantic haste to escape was playing right into his hands, Jake realized; still hunched low on the saddle, and taking advantage of every bit of tall cover, he urged the black on, pointing now even farther north.

He was ignoring the men working in and out of the brush well below him, as well as Denver Bannock, somewhere off to his left; he was concentrating instead on gaining the rock ledge capping the slope, and being there, waiting, when the outlaw reached it. Then would come the moment when he would exact the penalty for the crime that had been committed.

Lavendar, Richter, Sandman—and now Denver Bannock. That would leave only Pete Garret to bring to an accounting. Where could Garret be? He'd been lucky in finding Richter—a pure chance meeting. Lavendar's location had come from inquiry, as had Sandman's and Bannock's. He would find Garret by following that same course of asking questions, and he'd start just as soon as he'd taken care of the outlaw-turned-rancher. Somewhere along the line he'd come up with the answer—one he just might get from Bannock.

The gelding broke out onto a small, flinty meadow, slowed, sucking hard for wind. Jake allowed the horse to rest while he placed his gaze on the high ledge now less than a quarter of a mile to his left. Bannock, taking the more direct route, would probably be there by that moment, but that aroused no great concern in Harper. He had planned to reach the summit first, but the trail he'd been forced to follow had swung wide and thus caused delay.

It was of no consequence. Let the outlaw, entrenched in the rocks and keeping a sharp watch on the slope below him where he expected trouble to appear, convince himself that he was safe; coming in on the man from behind would pose no chore, and would be equally effective.

Sounds along the lower part of the slope drew Jake's attention, and he cast a quick glance to that direction. The crackling in the brush seemed nearer. It could only mean that not all of Bannock's riders were combing the area farther south, that some were working upslope toward the bluff. Harper's jaw tightened. He must act soon, or he'd have more than just the outlaw to deal with.

Shifting his gaze to the ledge, glistening in the golden light of the lowering sun, Jake gauged its distance from him and the probable location of Bannock. A bulging shoulder of scattered rock and thick brush overlooked the slope. It was an ideal point from which a man, holed up, could guard his back trail.

Fixing its location in mind, Jake roweled the black, set him in motion for a pine tree standing like a solitary sentinel in the rocks on Bannock's blind side. He glanced to the west; there was not much time left, but enough.

The gelding, breathing normally after his few moments' rest, climbed steadily, following a fairly distinct trail used by deer and other wildlife crossing the ridge. A short, tough grass covered the ground, muting the thud of the black's hooves, and Harper had no fear of his approach being noted by the outlaw.

But he was careful not to push his luck, and a short while later, as he drew near the ragged hogback, he pulled to a stop. The shoulder where he expected Bannock to be was just ahead and on the opposite side of the ridge. Swinging off the saddle, he tied the black to a clump of oak, and checking his pistol to be certain it was fully loaded, he began to work his way through the maze of boulders and springy brush.

He gained the crest. Pulling off his hat, he drew in

close and peered over its rim. A sigh of satisfaction slipped through him. The gray horse was just below him, reins anchored to a stump, and Denver Bannock, gun in hand, was hunched behind a large rock to the left of the shoulder, eyes fixed on the darkening grade below.

Cool, fully aware of the danger involved in moving in on a desperate outlaw already holding a weapon in his hand, Harper picked his way down the embankment to the ledge where Bannock was waiting. Not far below on the slope a man shouted something, provoking a reply from another one nearby. They were much too close.

Hat again brushed to the back of his head, Jake came to a halt a dozen strides from the outlaw. Arms hanging at his sides, he settled himself squarely on his feet. The sun was now gone behind the last range of hills, and there was only a pale yellow glare in the sky to silhouette him.

"Bannock . . ."

At the flat, challenging sound of Harper's voice, the outlaw sprang erect, whirled. His eyes spread wide in surprise, and his mouth gaped.

"You! How'd you get up here without me—"

"Came the long way," Jake said coldly, cutting in on the man's frantic rush of words. "Just like the law's had to take the long way to get you."

"Law! You ain't the law!"

"The law's the law, no matter how you look at it, and you're going to pay for breaking it."

Bannock glanced wildly about. "You're . . . you're crazy—plumb loony! You ain't got no right doing this!"

"That's a lie, Denver, and you know it. You and the

rest of your bunch killed that miner and his wife in cold blood, stole their money, and lied your way out of it."

"Wasn't proved."

"Maybe not, thanks to that slick lawyer you hired, but we know better—both of us. We know you did it, and we both know you've got to pay."

"Law turned me loose," Bannock said, covertly glancing down the slope. "Same as it did Henry and the others."

"Not the law. A crooked judge did that. And that's why I'm here. I'm giving you a chance to go free again, only—"

"Me draw against you? That the chance you're giving me?" Bannock demanded incredulously. "I ain't that dumb."

"It's all you've got," Harper said dryly. "Better make the best of it. Richter got the same. So would Lavendar and Matt Sandman if—"

"You didn't give Matt no chance—putting a knife in his back like you did!"

"Wasn't me that killed him. Somebody got to him and Lavendar ahead of me, but it's different with you. Found you, same as I will Pete Garret, in time to make you pay up. . . . You want to holster that iron you're holding and start from scratch, or you hanging on to it? All the same to me."

Bannock brushed at the sweat collected on his forehead, making no move with the right, in which he clutched the pistol, and once more glanced down the slope.

"Wasting your time if you're hoping some of your crew'll show up. They got off on the wrong trail."

"That's what you say," Bannock replied, with no real conviction in his voice. "Lige and them'll be here.

Like as not, they're throwing down on you right now from the brush."

"Don't count on Lige. He's back at the house. Took a shot at me, and I had to put a bullet in him. Rest are too far off to do you any good. Yell out if you don't believe me."

"Up here! Buck ... Akeman ... somebody! Up here on the ridge!"

Denver Bannock wasted no time taking up Jake's suggestion, and as the words echoed hollowly along the rocks, he listened anxiously for a response. It came, a faint halloo from far in the distance. The outlaw again mopped away the sweat on his face, shook his head helplessly.

Harper watched him in his cold, impersonal way. "Just you and me, Denver—nobody else. Let's get it over with."

"Wait a minute!" the outlaw cried. "Seems there ought to be something I can do to satisfy you. I ... I'm admitting to all you said about them killings and the robbery, and I'm real sorry you got sent to the pen for shooting Jim Rooney. That's what this here's all about, ain't it, you getting locked up for all that time?"

"Got nothing to do with it. I'm wanting you to answer up to the law for murder."

"Hell, man, I can't believe that! Ain't nobody figures the law's that important. Now, I'm willing to make it right with you, pay you for them years you was inside the pen. What do you say to a thousand dollars a year? That'd figure up to about three thousand, wouldn't it?"

"You ready?" Harper's voice was cold as winter's wind.

"I've done pretty good ranching," Bannock rushed

on desperately. "I'll up it to two thousand—that'll tot six thousand—in gold!"

"Use that gun, Denver, because I'm going to kill you anyway."

The outlaw threw himself forward, brought up his arm fast. Harper, scarcely moving, drew and fired. The bullet struck Bannock in the chest, dead center, drove him to the ground before he could trigger his weapon.

~ 17 ~

As the report of the gunshot rocked back and forth along the buttes and canyons, Jake Harper coolly lifted his weapon, flipped open the loading gate, and punched out the spent cartridge. Then, taking a shell from a belt loop, he reloaded the forty-five and slipped it back into its holster.

Glancing downslope, he started toward the prostrate outlaw, paused slightly when he saw a rider at the edge of the trees sitting motionless on his saddle, watching. And then, as the rider began slowly to climb the slope, plainly indicating that he had no desire to cut himself in on the situation, Jake continued. Reaching Bannock, he hunched beside the outlaw, who stared up at him with a steady hatred burning in his eyes.

"Hope . . . by God . . . you're satisfied . . ."

Harper nodded. "The law is. Leaves only Pete Garret. Where'll I find him?"

Bannock stirred. "Go to hell. If you figure I'll turn a hand to—"

"Why not? You're dying, and there's no reason why you should have to pay up and Garret go free."

The outlaw moved his head slightly. "Surer'n hell ain't about to do you no favor."

"Up to you. I'll track him down sooner or later."

Sweat was standing out in patches on the outlaw's face, and his eyes were taking on a glazed look. He struggled to focus them on Harper's bleak, unforgiving features.

"Yeh, expect you will."

"Counting you, all the gang've paid except Pete. Why let him get away?"

Jake shifted his attention to the rider. He had climbed to the ledge, halted at its rim, and was looking at Bannock. Evidently he had witnessed the shootout, but he would have been too far away to hear any of what was said.

Harper considered the man thoughtfully. "This here's a private matter," he said quietly. "Be making a bad mistake if you try taking a hand in it."

The rider nodded. "Seen it—Mr. Bannock had the edge. Still wasn't enough. He dead?"

"Almost."

"Harper . . ."

At the outlaw's low-voiced summons, Jake brought his attention back to the man. "Yeh?"

"Pete—he's in Orov . . ."

Harper bent lower, endeavored to hear the faltering words. It was of no use. Denver Bannock was dead.

Jake pulled himself upright. He'd heard enough. Pete Garret was in Oroville. At the last moment, Bannock had decided that Garret should be made to pay, even as had he and the remaining members of the outlaw gang.

"Mind telling me who you are, mister?"

At the cowhand's bluntly put question, Jake turned to him. "Name's Harper."

"There some kind of a grudge between you and the boss?"

"Could say that. Goes back a few years. Just now getting it settled. . . . You look after him?"

"Reckon so. I'm waiting for the rest of the boys to show up, after hearing that shot. They can give me a hand."

Harper pivoted slowly, hesitated. "You know a man called Pete Garret?" he asked. It was possible the outlaw had at some time visited Bannock.

The puncher clawed at the stubble covering his chin. In the near-dark he looked dusty, tired.

"Nope, can't say as I do, but I ain't been around these parts for long. Why?"

There was suspicion in the man's tone. Jake shrugged, moved on. "Just asking," he said.

Reaching the black, he stepped up onto the saddle and cut back to the game trail. Other Bannock riders were now gaining the top of the slope and joining the first cowhand, all shouting questions.

Harper listened idly as the gelding picked his way downgrade through the shadows. *What happened? Who shot Mr. Bannock? Why? Said his name was Harper. Was some kind of a grudge. Must've been that galoot they're hunting in town, one that knifed Matt Sandman. One of the boys that rode in for supplies was telling about it. Got Matt in the back. Nothing like that here. Harper let the boss draw his gun first and still beat him.*

The voices faded. Jake stared into the darkened corridors and cleared spaces between the trees, seeing nothing now but the blackness of the night that covered the slope. There was no point in going back to Junction City; he was a wanted man there. Bannock had said Pete Garret was in Oroville, and settling with the last of the outlaw bunch came first, before all else. Once that was done, he'd feel free to return and clear himself of the murder charge now hanging over his head.

Too, he would need to be on watch for U.S. Deputy Marshal Caleb Lynch, undoubtedly released from his embarrassing predicament by now, and brimming with hate and anger, searching for him. Jake wasn't proud of what he had done to the old lawman, but he'd had no choice. If he had simply left Lynch there, perhaps tied to a tree, the posse would have shortly found him, and then the marshal and the mounted party could have gotten quickly on his trail.

He could expect to be the object of Caleb Lynch's wrath for the remainder of his life, and also plan on the lawman redoubling his efforts to convict him of Matt Sandman's murder and thus put him back in Big Lonesome—if not sending him to the gallows. But he'd not lose any sleep over that; Lynch would confine his activities to the Junction City area, while he would be in Oroville, so it should not be difficult to avoid him. Jake didn't want a showdown with the marshal, but of course he would not sidestep it should it come to pass.

Word from Bannock that Pete Garret lived in Oroville had come as a bit of luck, as well as something of a surprise. He'd made inquiries while in the settlement, had found no one that knew the outlaw; but it could be that he'd, by sheer chance, asked persons who were not acquainted with the man. Jake shrugged at that thought. Such was hardly likely; in a small town like Oroville everyone not only knew everybody else but their business as well!

There was only one conclusion to be reached, Harper decided, thinking that over. Either Pete Garret had only recently moved into Oroville and was yet somewhat of a stranger, or he was living under a different name. Garret was the one he'd used at the trial; it was entirely possible it was false and he had now resumed his true identity.

It was fortunate, also, that the outlaw was in Oroville and not Junction City; problems encountered there in searching out the outlaw would have been endless. Now all he need do was bypass the settlement, ride on to Oroville. Chances were better than good he'd reach the town ahead of reports advising of Sandman and Bannock's deaths, and thus the likelihood of Garret panicking and making a run for it were small.

This time he'd not quit until he'd found the outlaw and settled with him. When that was done, he'd make the trip back to Junction City and quietly, under cover, dig into Sandman's death before he reported to the town's lawman. He'd concentrate on that woman—Cameo. She was the guilty one, Jake was certain, but it would be up to him to prove it, since the townspeople seemed to have their minds made up otherwise.

The cluster of buildings denoting the Bannock ranch, several windows, squared with yellow lamplight, was just ahead. Harper veered the tired black well away from them. He just might encounter some of the hired hands, be challenged as a trespasser, and at that stage of the game he wanted no additional trouble from any source.

He rode equally clear of the settlement. Undoubtedly the posse that had been looking for him had by that hour returned and called it quits for the night, but he could run into some civic-minded citizen who would recognize him, set up an alarm, and put the town's marshal and his volunteer lawmen on his trail again. And of course, he couldn't ignore the fact that Caleb Lynch was somewhere in the vicinity.

~ 18 ~

The warmness of the sun beating down upon his face awoke Jake Harper. For a long minute he lay perfectly still, eyes only partly open, as some inner instinct warned him that all was not well. And then he heard the jeering voice of Caleb Lynch.

"Get up, killer!"

Harper came fully alert, a surge of anger at his own dereliction racing through him. He had let down his guard, allowed himself to oversleep, and it was going to cost him dearly. Grim, he pulled himself to a sitting position, studied the pinched visage of the old lawman squatting on his heels safely beyond arm's reach.

"That gun and belt," Lynch said roughly. "Take it off and toss it to me. Lay a finger on the trigger, and I'll blow your goddamn head off! Was mighty tempted to, anyhow, you sprawled out there like you was, dead to the world."

Wordless, Harper complied, careful to do just as the marshal directed. A hard, pride-born fury was raging within Caleb Lynch, he knew, and it would take very little to provoke the man; accordingly, it was only smart to go along with the lawman's demands and hope to calm him down before he lost his head and did something drastic.

"Wasn't looking for you, marshal," Jake said, settling back.

"Reckon you wasn't!" Lynch snarled. "And I'm betting you were hoping plenty we'd not be meeting again after that stunt you pulled on me! Ought to've made you pay for that while you was laying there asleep. Ain't sure yet why I didn't . . . or don't right now."

"Probably because of that star you're wearing," Harper said, choosing his words carefully. "Being a federal lawman means something special."

"A hell of a lot you know about something like that! You ain't nothing but a back-stabbing killer and a gunslinger that takes advantage of others he knows ain't fast as he is."

"That means you know about Denver Bannock."

"Does. I was in the town marshal's office when some cowhands brought in his body."

"Then you know it was a fair shootout."

"Sure I know, only I'm knowing, too, that he didn't have no chance against you. Was murder, no matter how you slice it."

Jake's shoulders moved indifferently. "He was all but pointing his gun at me when I fired. Can't give a man a better edge than that. . . . How'd you find me?"

"Hunch . . . and tracking you. Hell, a blind-drunk squaw could've followed your trail. And then there was that sodbuster and his woman. Figured right then you was heading back to Oroville. . . . Was, wasn't you?"

"What I had in mind."

"Well, get yourself up and on your horse. Taking you there suits me good as any other town."

Harper sighed quietly, relieved that he was not

being returned to Junction City. Garret would be found in Oroville, and while his activities would be restricted to a cell in Jess Dakin's jail, he would have some opportunity of making inquiries concerning the outlaw.

Rising, Jake moved to the black. Tightening the cinch and buckling the bridle into place, he led the big horse to where the lawman waited.

"Like to know what you're taking me in for."

"For murder, goddamnit! For stabbing Matt Sandman in the back. Ain't no need of you asking that!"

"Just wanted to be sure," Harper said mildly. "Happens I didn't kill him. Like I've told you, he was dead when I got there. My guess is that woman, Cameo, did it."

"So you was claiming!"

"Except I can prove it when I get the chance," Jake continued, swinging onto the saddle.

"And I reckon you'd like me to turn you loose right here and now, let you head back to that town and start proving it—only that ain't what you'd do. You'd line out straight for the border—that's what you'd do!"

"Hardly," Jake Harper said quietly. "Not about to spend the rest of my life dodging bounty hunters and lawmen like you."

"You ain't going to get the chance," Lynch said, grinning. "Now, move out. You know the road into town, and don't make no wrong moves. I'll be right behind you, just honing to shoot you for trying to escape. Way I see it, cutting you down'd be a mighty big favor to the country, so it's best you don't give me no reasons."

It was late in the morning when they reached the settlement. Harper, under the gruff directions of the old lawman who, with pistol drawn and ready, was a horse's length behind him, rode down the center of the main street and halted at the rack in front of the jail.

Their appearance drew immediate attention. Shoppers along the sidewalks paused to stare, storeowners and other businessmen came out for closer looks, and Jake noticed Seera Lavendar, in company with the drummer who seemed to spend a great deal of time hanging around her, emerge from the hotel and take a stand on the porch. It all brought a wry grin to Harper's lips; he hadn't realized Caleb Lynch was such a show-off.

Dakin, the sheriff, appeared in the doorway of his office and jail almost at once, paused to frown, and then advanced to the hitchrack.

"What's this, marshal?"

"Man that murdered Matt Sandman, down in Junction City. Going to have to lodge him in one of your cells till I can sort of arrange things," Lynch replied, dismounting and shaking his head as if he faced a most vexing problem. "He's a bad one."

"Same jasper that shot it out with that gambler, ain't he?" Dakin observed, drawing his pistol to aid Lynch, now motioning for Jake to come off the black.

"The same."

"How's it happen you didn't put the cuffs on him? Seems you'd be taking a mighty long chance . . ."

"He knowed better'n try anything on me," the marshal said with a tight smile.

Dakin wagged his head doubtfully. Then: "What was the deal on this Sandman?"

"Harper here stuck a knife in his back. Then he went out and shot down a rancher—euchred him into drawing on him, same as he done that gambler. . . . Get inside," he added to Jake, gesturing with his pistol.

Harper, finished with winding the black's reins about the crossbar of the rack, stepped up onto the landing of the jail. A fair-sized crowd had quickly collected, and pausing, he swept it with a probing glance. Pete Garret could be among them. Behind him he heard Sheriff Dakin's voice, filled with resentment.

"As soon you'd took him back to Junction City instead of locking him up in my jail. Was there he done the killing. Just don't figure it's my responsibility to have to look after him."

"Ain't much of a jail they got there—only a cracker box—and feeling was running a mite high. That rancher—name was Bannock—and Sandman, they was well-liked."

"Ain't got much more'n a cracker box here," Dakin grumbled.

There were no familiar faces in the crowd, Jake saw. If Garret was living in Oroville, he was either absent from the settlement at the moment or taking pains to keep out of sight. Harper shrugged, winced as he felt the muzzle of Lynch's gun jab into his spine, and moved on across the square of planks and entered the jail.

"Cell's through there," Dakin said, pointing to a hallway leading off the rear of the office, and pushing by, led the way.

Harper, the thought of again being caged filling him with a tightness, followed the sheriff slowly, barely aware of the steady pressure of Caleb Lynch's gun muzzle against his back. Once the iron grille door of a cell slammed behind him, there would be very little he could do. Perhaps he had looked at it wrong; maybe it would have been better if Lynch had taken him back to Junction City.

There he would have had a chance to talk matters

over with that town's lawman, persuade him to look into the possibility that it had been Matt Sandman's woman, Cameo, who had plunged a knife into the saloon man.

Now he was in a position to do nothing but wait, sweat it out. Dakin, the Oroville lawman, would care nothing about his problem—that of being innocent of the murder charge—and probably wouldn't even bother to listen. In Dakin's mind he was a killer, such assumption being based on the Yancey Richter shootout; therefore, any and all of the Junction City claims were undoubtedly true.

Like as not, Caleb Lynch had figured it that way, had deliberately made a point of not taking him back to Junction City, so that he could do nothing whatsoever about the charges leveled against him. Harper swore silently. He had preferred coming to Oroville because of Pete Garret; now he was not so sure it was smart.

Moving past Dakin, standing at the entrance of one of the cells, he stepped inside, flinched as the barred door slammed shut and the key grated in the lock.

"Reckon that'll hold him," he heard Lynch say in a satisfied voice.

"Sure ought. . . . How long you aiming to keep him here?" Dakin asked, wheeling about, the ring of keys in his hand.

"Well, can't say for sure. . . ."

"Don't much like the idea," the sheriff went on, disgruntled. "He ain't the town's responsibility, and if a bunch of them hotheads from Junction City show up with a rope, aiming to bust him out and string him up, I—"

"You leave me worry about that," Lynch broke in confidently. "Can handle anything that comes up, and

I'll get him out of here soon's I can. Aim to fetch him back to Higgtown, turn him over to the warden again for safekeeping. He's a real loony."

"Again? Was he in the pen?"

"Sure was. Got sent there for a killing, but he worked around, got hisself pardoned. Bad thing about it all is that he was a lawman once, but he went sour and a little crazy. Thinks he's got a call to kill off every man that he figures broke the law—whether he did or not. . . . Come on, let's set a spell. I'll tell you all about Mr. Jake Harper."

⌁ 19 ⌁

Harper, standing in the center of his cage, listened to the marshal's words with a wry sort of humor stirring through him, and then, as the door leading into Sheriff Jess Dakin's office closed and he could hear no more, he turned his attention to the cell.

It was built into a corner of the building, the interior sides of iron bars, the outer being the walls of the structure itself. A single window covered by heavy steel mesh was placed in the center of the north side, and was well above the board floor.

Jake gave the nonexistent escape possibilities a few minutes' thought, and then, dragging the slat cot upon which lay a rumpled wool blanket to a place below the window, he climbed onto the narrow, platformlike affair and peered through the small squares of the grating.

The crowd was still in front of the jail. He could see most of the persons making up the gathering, all standing about talking among themselves. Again he scanned the faces available to him, once more recognized no one as Pete Garret. He wondered then if the dying Denver Bannock had deliberately given him a false lead. It could be that the last member of the outlaw

134

gang actually lived elsewhere, and Bannock was having his measure of bitter revenge.

Regardless, Jake realized, he could not permit himself to remain cooped up in Oroville's two-bit jail on a charge of which he was not guilty. He'd had no choice earlier but to let Caleb Lynch bring him in; the old lawman was on edge, and the slightest bit of opposition would have been tantamount to dropping a lighted match into a keg of gunpowder.

But that was past now. Lynch had cooled off, and the danger of getting a bullet in the head from him was over for the time being. The problem currently to be faced was how to break out of the jail, regain his freedom, and go on about the business of finding Pete Garret. When that was accomplished and he'd settled with the outlaw, then he'd return to Junction City— without Caleb Lynch—and get things straightened out.

Turning, Jake stepped down from the cot, began to make a more thorough investigation of the cell, examining its corners, the bars, the door, and its lock and hinges. He could hear the mutter of voices in the adjoining office, where Lynch was apparently still recounting his life to Jess Dakin, no doubt emphasizing the claim that he was a deadly killer, a loony who believed it was his bounden duty to take the law into his own hands—become a one-man vigilante committee, as the lawman had said before.

Loony—hell! He was simply carrying out the letter of the law, finishing up a job that had gotten sidetracked that day in court when Judge Amos Chancellor, turning his back on honesty, had turned five outlaws loose to go their way.

The cell was tight, showed signs of having been tested by previous prisoners. Harper stepped back onto the cot, put his attention on the mesh covering the window. The heavy-gauge metal was firmly embedded in a band of concrete that formed a frame. It, too, bore evidence of futile tampering. Jake again dropped to the floor, and dragging the cot back to its place against the adjacent wall, settled down. Brushing at the sweat on his face, he swore quietly. Jess Dakin's claim that his jail was no more than a cracker box had been a misstatement, one made merely for effect. No forcible escape from the cell was possible; a man would have to utilize some means other than a breakout.

Noon passed, and the day wore on, hot and stuffy within the jail. Jake heard the two lawmen depart, the thump of their boot heels a hollow beat on the wooden floor, was aware of their return an hour or so later.

Elsewhere in the settlement a blacksmith worked at his trade, anvil ringing methodically. Dogs barked now and then, and riders traversed the nearby main street. Somewhere among the houses a child cried pitifully, continually, victim of an ailment, no doubt, and once a gunshot rolled across the flats to echo through the still air.

Around midafternoon, with Harper still probing his mind ceaselessly for an idea that would lead to escape, the inner door swung open, and Caleb Lynch, a sly grin on his lips, looked in.

"Figured you'd like to know," he said, leaning against the frame. "I'm taking you back to Higgtown, come morning. Decided that was the best place for you."

Jake studied the lawman coldly. "Man has to be guilty of committing a crime to get sent there. I'm not."

"You are far as I'm concerned, and I reckon the same goes for them folks down in Junction City.

Anyways, it won't make no difference. Big Lonesome's where you belong."

"Going to be a little hard explaining to the warden—"

"Naw, no trouble at all. He's a good friend of mine, and when I tell him what you've been doing, he's going to be real happy to turn you over to them guards."

"Man can't be locked up in the pen without first being tried. That's his right—"

"You ain't got no rights, not no more," the old lawman said pointedly. "Be bringing you your victuals about dark. Sheriff's leaving. I'll be looking out for you."

Lynch withdrew, the hard, ironic smile still on his weathered face. Jake settled back, the prospect of being taken to the high-walled prison on the hill outside Higgtown now heightening his determination to escape.

Caleb Lynch could do it, he knew. Working with the warden, it would be a simple matter for the marshal to have him locked up again, a nameless nonentity not appearing on the prison's records, excommunicated from the outside world with no hope of ever being released.

Why was Lynch returning him to Big Lonesome? Why wasn't the lawman following the usual procedure and taking him back to Junction City or to the territorial capital, where he could be tried in the usual manner for the murder of Matt Sandman—which was the only charge that could be mustered against him? There was only one answer to that question: Caleb Lynch was taking personal vengeance upon him and was unwilling to let him stand before a judge because he feared the man he'd come to hate would be able to prove his innocence.

Likely Jess Dakin, Oroville's sheriff, was unaware of Lynch's scheme, probably believed the deputy marshal intended to move his prisoner to where he would be accorded a fair trial. But Jake realized he could forget trying to talk with Dakin, make him understand what was going on and that he was becoming a part of it. The sheriff had left town, would be gone perhaps for days, leaving it all in Caleb Lynch's hands.

He must come up with something, and do so before the night was gone. Harper began to move slowly about in his cell, mind centered on the problem. After a time, sweat beading his forehead, he sat down on the cot. It would be foolish to hold off until Lynch started back to Higgtown with him, believing there would come an opporunity for escape. He could be sure the old lawman would have him in both leg irons and handcuffs.

Slumped on the cot, shoulders pressed against the wall, Jake continued to probe the possibilities as the afternoon dragged by. Only one thing was absolutely clear in his mind; Caleb Lynch or no other man was going to put him back inside Big Lonesome—not alive.

Finally he rose, thoughtfully turned his attention to the cot, a crude makeshift of wooden slats nailed to a heavy, oblong framework and with short lengths of two-by-fours for legs. Listening briefly and hearing no sounds in the office, Harper pulled the cot away from the wall, and holding it motionless by placing a foot upon it, wrenched one of the back legs free.

A glow of satisfaction running through him, he returned the bed to its place along the wall, wedging it tight so that the missing leg would not be noticeable. Resuming his seat, this time at the opposite end of the arrangement in order to prevent any sagging, he settled down to wait. He was feeling considerably better now; at least he had a weapon of sorts that could be used if an opportunity presented itself.

It came at mealtime.

Hunched on the cot, the length of wood thrust under the right leg of his pants, where it was not visible, Harper looked up as the door opened abruptly. Caleb Lynch, a tray covered by a somewhat soiled dish towel, stepped into the room.

"About time," Jake grumbled. "Last grub I had was at that homesteader's."

Lynch grinned, obviously enjoying Harper's declared discomfort.

"Just keep setting where you are," he said. "Make a wrong move, and I'll throw these here victuals to the dogs."

Jake folded his arms across his knees. Eyes narrowed, he watched in silence as the lawman, balancing the tray in one hand, a ring of keys in the other, crossed to the cell's door and opened the lock.

"Warning you again," Lynch said cautiously. "Don't try nothing!"

Harper remained motionless, but within him tension had built itself to wire-tautness. This would be his chance—likely the only one; he had to make the most of it.

"Had them rustle up some steak and fried spuds for you," Lynch said, advancing into the cage. "Got some biscuits and coffee, too. Figured a man headed for where you're going had a square meal coming—sort of like the one a fellow gets just before they hang him."

"Taking that as a real favor, marshal," Jake said dryly.

"Figured you would," Lynch replied, equally dry.

"Get back there against the wall while I set this tray on the cot."

Harper came erect slowly, careful not to disturb the precarious balance of the three-legged framework, and moved to the side. Lynch, hanging the ring of keys on the butt of his holstered pistol, advanced farther into the cell, bent forward to relieve himself of the tray.

Instantly Jake Harper, raising his leg slightly, snatched up the length of oak. Quick as a striking rattler, he lashed out. The club caught the lawman on the top of his head, dropped him to the floor with a noisy clattering of tinware.

Taut, Harper reached down, yanked the marshal's pistol from its holster, and hurrying to the still-open connecting door, listened. There was no one in the sheriff's office; Lynch had come alone.

Wheeling, Jake reentered the cell, and picking up the dish towel, tore it into strips. With one he drew a tight gag over the lawman's mouth, and then with those remaining, bound the man's arms and legs, linking them together in such manner that Lynch could not move about. That done, Harper dragged the unconscious lawman into a corner, and taking the ring of keys, stepped out of the cell, closed the iron grille door, and locked it.

Cool, thorough, he crossed to the inner entrance, shut and secured it also before turning to the desk standing in the center of the office. Pulling open the drawers, he searched about until he located his own belt and gun, strapped them on, and then dropped back to the window and glanced out.

Shadows were beginning to fill the street, almost deserted this near to supper hour. He would have no trouble leaving the building, but caution would not permit his taking a risk. Best to use the rear exit. With

Sheriff Dakin gone from the settlement and Lynch in no position to call for help or free himself, he could have hours of daylight yet in which to seek out Pete Garret, if he were careful.

Closing the front door of the jail, he tried the keys until he found the proper one, turned the lock, and then hurried back down the narrow hallway to the rear of the structure. The thick slab panel with its strap-iron hinges and cross-braces was locked, and again by trial and error he fitted keys until he found the one that released the bolt. Stepping out into the weedy area behind the building, Jake secured the door, tossed the ring into a nearby horse trough, and turned toward the Cattleman's Hotel.

Not wanting to waste even a moment in consideration, he had already decided to go first to the hostelry and have a talk with Seera Lavendar. It was possible her pa had made some mention of Pete Garret in letters to her; or, if not, he'd insist she permit him to look through the outlaw's papers. There had to be a trace of Garret somewhere.

⤙ 20 ⤚

The smell of wood smoke coming from cook-stove chimneys was a pleasant perfume hanging in the warm, quiet air as Jake Harper strode down the alley-way behind the structures on the west side of Oroville's main street. He would again enter the hotel by its back door and thus avoid the attention of any who might be abroad on the sidewalks.

He progressed at a steady pace, keeping close to the store buildings, wading through piles of trash and other debris, circling stacks of cord wood, empty crates, packing boxes and kegs, arriving finally at the rear of the Cattleman's, designated simply by the word HOTEL painted on the wall.

Glancing around to make certain he had covered the distance from the jail unobserved, and seeing no one, Harper stepped up to the door, entered the now-familiar corridor that led to the lobby, lying in dark silence, and pressed forward to that front area.

"Is there something?"

At the question coming unexpectedly from his left, Jake Harper turned. It was Seera Lavendar. She had been sitting behind the desk reading, and in the dim light of the lobby where he was standing, she had not immediately recognized him. Now, as he faced her and his identity became clear, a tightness gathered her features into severe lines.

"It's you," she murmured. "They've let you go. I should've expected that."

Harper only shrugged. He would make no explanation, even if he were so inclined, as her scorn for him—for a country that permitted killers, such as she believed him to be, to run loose—was apparent.

"Said before I have no vacancies."

"Not looking for a room," Jake said coolly. "Only information."

Seera studied him with unbending distaste. "I don't know what kind of information I could give you."

"Trying to find a man. He was a friend of your pa's. Was told he lived here in Oroville."

Her eyes, their blue almost black in the meager light of a bracket lamp on the wall behind her, did not waver.

"So that you can murder him?"

Harper's jaw hardened. "Haven't murdered anybody yet—not ever in my life."

"Then what do you call it when you shoot down somebody like that Mr. Richter, and that rancher, not to mention the man who ran that place in the next town—Sandman, I think his name was. You stabbed him."

"No," Jake said patiently. "That wasn't me, and I aim to prove it. Far as Richter and the rancher were concerned, they had an even chance—better."

He was growing a bit weary of defending his actions to her. That she was from a part of the country where shootouts were unheard-of was no longer an excuse. The accepted custom of two men settling their differences with guns had been explained to her by that time, he was sure; and if the girl only knew it, she had no room to criticize and judge, having had Henry Lavendar, a back-shooting killer, for a father.

"Of course, you can justify anything if you look hard enough for a reason."

Harper stirred indifferently, unwilling to waste more time on the pointless argument. "Man I'm hunting's named Pete Garret."

"Why should I know him?"

"Told you. Was a friend of your pa's. They rode together and—"

"What do you know of my father?" Seera broke in stiffly.

"Probably a good deal more than you do. This Garret—did your pa ever mention him in his letters to you?"

The girl looked down. "He didn't write very often," she said, a bitterness in her voice. "Usually it was just a short note. He never mentioned anybody."

"There any other letters or papers I can look through? Might come across—"

"He had no papers—only the deed to this property. . . . I wouldn't let you see them if there were."

Harper swore under his breath. It was a dead end, but he was still convinced that Denver Bannock had spoken the truth with his last breath.

"You certain you've never heard the name?"

"No, I haven't. Why are you so insistent on finding him? Is he another man you want to kill? I asked you that, but you didn't answer."

"Little matter of personal business," Harper said, and glanced toward the street as the sound of a passing rider drew his sharp attention.

It could be Sheriff Dakin returning from wherever he had been, and if so, Caleb Lynch would shortly be free and the lawmen would start combing the town for him. But it was only a cowhand, slumped on his saddle as he made his way toward the Maricopa.

"Well, I can't help you," Seera declared abruptly, her tone softening somewhat. "My father never mentioned a Pete Garret, and I've never heard of him. . . . That man Sandman—you say you didn't kill him?"

"No. He was dead when I walked into his office."

"But you went there to shoot him."

Jake remained silent, neither affirming nor denying.

"Isn't that what they locked you up for?"

"That and a couple other reasons," he said, and glanced again through the lobby window. Two more riders heading for the saloon after a hard day working the range.

Seera's face was puzzled. "Then, if they think you killed him and put you in jail for it, what are you doing out?"

"Looking for Pete Garret," Harper said blandly. "If it means anything to you, as soon as I find Garret, I'm riding back to Junction City to clear things up."

The girl was staring fixedly at him. "You mean you've broken out of jail?"

"About the size of it."

"Then I've got to get word to the sheriff—"

"Don't bother trying. He's out of town, and like I've said, I'm turning myself in to the law at Junction City after I find Garret."

Seera nodded slowly. "Yes, I believe you will," she said, a faint note of admiration stealing into her voice. "If this Garret isn't here, where will you go next?"

"Haven't figured that far ahead. Be trying the next

town, I reckon, and then the one after that if he isn't there. But I'm not giving up on him being here yet."

"I suppose it's possible. I've been here only a short while, and there're lots of people I haven't met or gotten to know. Maybe Garret works on one of the ranches or has a place of his own and does his trading in town. What does he look like?"

There was genuine interest in the girl's tone. He studied her closely, the gentle beauty of her regular features touching him. And the thought *How could she be the daughter of Henry Lavendar?* passed through his mind.

"Been almost three years since I saw him," he said, returning to her question. "He'd be in his late thirties. Was small-framed, wiry, had sandy hair and sort of pale eyes—light blue, I expect they were."

Seera gave that consideration. "Sounds familiar, but I suppose a lot of men would fit that description," she said finally. "I . . . I wish I could help you."

Jake Harper nodded, smiled, pleased that the girl's attitude toward him appeared to have changed. Maybe she was beginning to have some understanding of the country, of him.

"Appreciate that, and I'm obliged."

He would've liked to ask her to say she had not seen him if Dakin or Caleb Lynch later made inquiries for him, but he was unwilling to suggest that she lie. In all probability she would refuse, and he guessed he could not blame her.

Touching the brim of his hat, he turned, started for the hallway. He'd drop back to the livery barn, where Dakin had likely stabled the black, get out of town, and find a spot where he could do some thinking without fear of being caught again by the law.

"Hope to see you again," he said, and drew to a sudden halt, attention once more on the street.

A man, coming from somewhere up the way, was walking briskly along the board path fronting the opposite row of store buildings. There was something vaguely familiar in the way he carried himself—the forward set of his shoulders, the motionless hanging of the hands, which seemed to be hovering at his sides.

"Who's that?" Harper asked, abruptly tense.

Seera glanced through the open doorway. "Mr. Parsons," she replied. "Owns the gun shop over there."

"Maybe that's what he's calling himself now," Harper said quietly, moving toward the hotel's entrance, "but that's Pete Garret."

Seera, eyes troubled, watched Jake Harper, moving in a quiet, gliding sort of way, step out onto the hotel's gallery and pause, shoulder pressed against one of the roof supports. A casualness had come over him, almost an indifferent ease, but she knew he was studying Parsons sharply, and missing nothing.

She'd met the gun-shop owner only once. It had been in the Kansas Pride Restaurant, and she had not cared for him. There was something sly and secretive about the man, and someone had told her—Sheriff Dakin, she thought it was—that he had been involved with her father in business deals. But so also were other men around town, and she had thought nothing of it. That he could be the Pete Garret that Jake Harper was seeking, however, was easily possible.

Fascinated, she continued to watch Harper. He was perfectly still, yet there was a poised quality to him, like a coiled spring awaiting only the slightest pressure to release it. A throb of regret swept through her. Why did he have to be the sort of man he was—a killer, a gunman, a person who seemingly thought no more of taking another's life than he did of brushing off a fly?

He was everything a man should be—strong, honest, intelligent, handsome in a rugged kind of way; and she could not deny that she was attracted to him, had been from the very start, despite the battle she had waged with herself.

If she were ever to take a husband, he would be the type—the one, actually—if only he wasn't what he was. She could never reconcile herself to accepting his values when it came to human life. Shooting a man down to settle an argument was utterly wrong.

Why couldn't Jake Harper have been like other men—a merchant of some kind, or an ordinary working man, or even a drummer like Casey Kunkle, who was still hanging around hoping for the chance to become better acquainted? But then, she guessed, Jake Harper wouldn't have been Jake Harper.

Marry him, though, she never could—not unless he changed and forgot about settling whatever differences he had with others by shooting it out with them; and even then she wasn't certain she could accept him because of the past that she knew behind him. The recollection of those few moments when he stopped the stagecoach, made them all get out, and then forced that man, Richter, into drawing his weapon, were still vividly etched on her mind. Like as not she'd relive them every time she saw him talking to some man, and be wondering if he was about to engage in another duel to the death.

Seera pulled herself from her thoughts. Parsons had reached his shop, had turned in, and was unlocking the door. Jake was slowly drawing himself away from the roof support, coming erect. Had he decided Parsons was a stranger, after all?

In that next moment, she had her answer. Jake Harper stepped down from the porch into the loose dust, and arms hanging loosely at his sides, was starting across the street.

21

There was no doubt the man known in Oroville as Parsons was Pete Garret. Harper had come to that conclusion when he stepped off the porch of the hotel, and taking advantage of the thick-trunked cottonwood growing at the edge of the walk in front of the gun shop, angled toward it.

Garret had noticed him, Jake was certain, but whether he'd been recognized was a matter of conjecture. It was likely; he had, after a few moments' scrutiny, known the outlaw for who he was, and it was only logical to assume Garret would remember him.

Taut, mind centered wholly on what lay ahead, minimizing the risk of his direct approach by keeping the cottonwood between himself and the building's entrance, Harper proceeded at a slow, relentless pace. He was not conscious of Seera Lavendar, now standing in the hotel's doorway, watching him closely, or of others along the street, arrested by his tall, stalking figure, who had paused to stare at him.

The window of the gun shop, its glass at first reflecting, mirrorlike, the sunlight, became transparent as Jake's angle of approach changed when he drew nearer. Beyond it he could see Garret moving about in his shop, making preparations of some sort.

Back at the end of town the bell in the steeple of the church began to toll, measuring out six echoing beats as it announced the time of day, and farther on, the thud of hooves and the rattle and creak of wood proclaimed the arriving of the north-bound stagecoach.

Harper drew to a stop. The door of the gun shop was open, and he could see the outline of the outlaw in its opening.

"All right, Pete...."

Garret moved forward slowly, emerging from the shadows, and took a stand on the walk. A pistol now hung at his side, the butt of the weapon rising high out of its holster in the manner favored by many gunfighters.

"You ain't getting no cinch with me, marshal," the outlaw said, folding his arms across his chest.

Jake settled himself squarely on his feet. Satisfaction was flowing through him like a cool, quiet stream. He'd found the last of the killers; the search was over. It would all end there in the dusty street of a town called Oroville, one way or another.

"Not a marshal anymore," he said. "You had a hand in changing that—you and the others."

"Just squaring up, then, that it?"

"No, finishing what the law started."

Garret frowned. His ruddy face had rounded somewhat during the years, but his eyes still had the same bleak flatness.

"That don't make no sense."

"Didn't to Bannock either, or Richter, but I don't aim to waste time trying to explain it to you.... When you're ready, go for your gun."

"Figured you was up to something like this when I

seen you around. . . . Could be you've made yourself a big mistake. I was always faster'n you."

"Could be," Harper said quietly. "Reckon we're about to find out."

A deep hush had settled over the street, and up in the direction of the jail there was activity of some sort. Jake did not take his eyes off the outlaw, knowing the man was deliberately trying to dull his reflexes by allowing the moments to drag, the tension to build. It was an old trick, brought a thin-lipped smile of contempt to Harper's face.

"Was just thinking," Garret said. "If you'd maybe looked me up first, Denver and Yancey and Matt Sandman might still be living instead of laying in the boneyard."

"Maybe. For the record, it wasn't me that got Sandman. He was dead when I found him, same as Lavendar."

"They wasn't much anyway," Garret said casually, and then abruptly he was moving.

His hand swept down. At the first break in his stance Harper went for the weapon at his side also. The guns came up, the two reports blending into one. Jake felt the searing burn of a bullet ripping through his upper arm, half-spun from the impact, caught himself, thumbed back the hammer of his forty-five for a second shot, hesitated.

Through a film of smoke he could see the outlaw, features drawn tight, twisting slowly about, pistol slipping from his hand. Somewhere along the street voices were yelling and figures were hurrying toward him; there was a grating of sand as iron-tired wheels cut into it, and the jangle of harness metal as the stage wheeled up to the hotel.

Garret pitched forward suddenly, sprawled face-down. Only then did Jake Harper's taut shape relent, and he became fully aware of his surroundings. Holstering his weapon, he glanced at the bloodstain spreading along his arm, reached for the neckerchief around his neck.

Seera Lavendar had come off the hotel's porch and was running up to him, her face chalk-white, and from the corner of an eye he saw Caleb Lynch, in the company of Sheriff Jess Dakin, approaching at a trot. The federal lawman's features were livid with anger.

"Jake . . . are you bad hurt?" Seera cried as she reached him.

He shook his head, looked beyond her. The stage had halted at the rack fronting the hotel, but the driver as well as the passengers were unmoving, were simply watching in mute surprise.

"Only nicked my arm," Harper said.

"Parsons is still alive!" a man shouted from near the sidewalk. "Somebody help me get him to the doc!"

"Fellow here needs patching up some too," another voice in the quickly growing crowd said. "Lean on me, Mr. Harper, I'll take you to Patterson's office."

Jake shook his head at the man. It was the drummer he'd seen in the hotel. "No rush. Expect the bleeding's already stopped."

"If you'll come with me," Seera Lavendar said, "I think I can take care of it."

"He ain't going nowhere!"

Caleb Lynch's harsh words brought a sigh to Harper's lips. He half-turned, faced the old lawman, nodded.

"Was expecting you, marshal, but not quite so soon. Was hoping to get down to Junction City and straighten out that murder charge before I saw you again."

"Like hell you was!" Lynch shouted. "And you got a jailbreak to answer for now. I—"

"You the fellow they was after for putting a knife in Matt Sandman?"

It was the stagecoach driver. He had swung down from his perch, was moving in through the crowd.

"That's him," Lynch snapped. "I'm taking him in for murder."

"No need," the driver said. "Just come from Junction City. Place is jumping with excitement. Woman there 'fessed up to killing Sandman. Seems he was quitting her for one of them other girls, calling off their getting hitched, and she got mad and stuck a knife in him."

Jake glanced at Lynch. The lawman, jaw set to a stubborn angle, was glaring at the driver.

"I ain't believing none of that."

"Don't have to take my word for it," the man said, jerking a thumb at the coach. "Half a dozen people setting there that'll tell you it's the truth."

Jess Dakin shrugged. "Rufe wouldn't lie," he said. "Ain't got no reason to. Reckon you been holding the wrong party, marshal."

There was no ebbing of the anger that gripped Caleb Lynch. "Still want him for hitting me over the head and breaking jail!" he said in a trembling voice.

"Except you'd best forget that, after what you put him through."

"No, by God—I ain't forgetting nothing!"

Dakin slid a look at the lawman, frowned, shook his head. Turning to Harper, he said, "Go along with the lady, let her fix up that arm. I'll do some talking to the marshal."

22

Harper, following Seera Lavendar and trailed by the drummer—Kunkle, somebody had called him— moved through the dispersing crowd and entered the hotel. The stage passengers had now dismounted, were also filing into the lobby and crossing to the desk, where they would make arrangements for a night's lodging.

The girl, pausing behind the counter, turned to Kunkle. "I'd appreciate it if you'd see to the registering while I take care of Jake's . . . Mr. Harper's wound."

The drummer nodded eagerly, immediately fell to the task, and Seera, continuing on, led Jake into her living quarters.

"I'll get some water and cloth for a bandage while you take off your shirt," she said, oddly reserved as she crossed the room to the stove.

Taking a pan, she filled it from a quietly simmering kettle, and obtaining a clean white cloth from the top drawer of a chiffonier, returned to where he waited, torso stripped to his undershirt.

"Don't amount to much," he said, looking at the ragged tear midway between shoulder and elbow. "Been hurt worse falling off a horse."

155

"I'll clean it," Seera said, "but you ought to let the doctor put something on it."

"Can drop by and see him later."

Seera wet the cloth, began to dab at the wound. "I heard what Parsons—or Garret—said out there in the street, and my father was mentioned. Was there a gang—"

"It's all over and done with now," Harper cut in, brushing aside the question.

"No, not for me, and it never will be until I know what it was all about. I . . . I have to know, Jake. . . . You set out deliberately to kill those men—Richter, that rancher, and Garret—and you did. You would have killed Sandman, too, only you didn't need to. Why?"

"They cheated the law. Killed a man and his wife, robbed them, and then got themselves a slick lawyer and lied their way out of it."

"And you were the lawman that caught them."

Harper nodded. "Ended up with them twisting things around before a judge who saw it their way. I went to the pen for two and a half years, while they went free."

"So when you were released, you set out to catch them, make them pay for what they'd done."

"Not to me—but to the law," Harper said quietly, watching her wrap a strip of the cloth about the wound, rip the end into tabs, and tie them together. "Was a promise I made to myself. Figured the law had to be upheld."

"You just took it on yourself to execute those men, even though this law you're so proud of found them not guilty."

"A judge did that—it wasn't the law. And they were guilty," Jake said coldly, pulling on his shirt and vest.

He nodded crisply. "Obliged to you for fixing me up."

Seera was studying him intently. "My father—that why you came to see him, because he was one of them?"

Harper was quiet for a long minute. Finally: "He was. Don't like telling you that, but—"

"You would have killed him, too?"

Again Jake was slow to reply. "I won't lie to you, Seera. I would've if he'd been alive."

The girl turned away, all the light going from her eyes. "I was afraid that was it after what I heard, but I kept hoping . . . praying that it wouldn't be true."

"I'd like to say I'm sorry," Harper said slowly, "and I reckon I am, far as your finding out about your pa's concerned—but not about him. He was no better than the others."

"And you would have shot him down just like you did them! I . . . I hardly knew him, but he was my father, and I don't think I could ever forget what you intended to do."

"Hardly expect you to, but I'd not lie to hide it."

"Maybe it would have been better. Then we could have had a life together." Seera paused, frowned, bit at her lower lip. "I mean, if we—"

"I know what you mean," he said gently. "Was starting to do some wishing myself, but it would have been wrong to begin on a lie. Thing like that festers. . . ."

"Oh, why did you have to be the way you are!" she cried, turning to him suddenly. "Why did you have to take it on yourself to be a judge and an executioner! It's made you a cold-blooded murderer! You kill because you think you're right, and maybe you even enjoy it!"

"Harper!"

Caleb Lynch's voice, coming from the street,

reached into the hotel's farthest corner. Jake's shoulders lifted, to form a straight line, as a hardness stiffened his features.

"You hear me, Harper? Get out here! We're settling this—now!"

Anxiety flooded Seera's eyes. "What does he mean? I thought the sheriff . . ."

"Seems he's decided to stay out of it," Harper said curtly, and wheeled to the door.

As he entered the small area behind the hotel's desk, Kunkle, the drummer, drawing aside to allow him room to pass, murmured something. Unhearing, Jake continued on across the lobby, halted at its entrance, and glanced out into the street.

Caleb Lynch was standing directly in front of the building, one hand resting on the pistol at his hip, the other clenching and unclenching as it hung at his side. The lawman's features were blood-red, and his eyes were small glowing coals beneath his overshadowing brows.

There was no sign of Jess Dakin, but two dozen or more persons were ranged along the walks, all carefully out of the line of fire. Harper stirred impatiently, stepped out onto the porch.

"What the hell's the matter with you, marshal?" he demanded.

"Ain't nothing wrong with me!" Lynch replied in a furious rush of words. "Just doing what I have to— putting a stop to your killing."

"You know that's a lie. Men I went after are all dead, and that ends it. I'm riding on, looking to start a new life somewhere."

"You ain't riding no place!" Lynch shouted. "I don't let nobody slap and shove me around the way you've done!"

A hard smile cracked Jake Harper's lips. "Reckon I know the real reason now why you're trying to make me draw on you. Forget it, marshal."

"By God, you'll stand and draw or—"

"I don't want to kill you, Lynch—and you know damn well I can."

"Maybe. I ain't so sure. Go for your gun!"

"The hell with you," Jake Harper said, and pivoting on a heel, put his back to the anger-shaken lawman.

Moving to the end of the porch, he stepped down, started for the alleyway at the rear of the building. He'd go to the stable, get his horse, and leave—put Oroville behind him. . . .

"Jake!"

It was Seera Lavendar's voice. Harper paused, came about.

"Jake, I was wrong!", the girl said, stopping at the edge of the gallery. "I realized that when I saw you refuse to shoot that old man. I'm sorry. . . ."

"No need. Expect it's all a bit hard for you to understand."

"I don't care if I ever do. I just know I want to be with you . . . go wherever you go."

"You've got yourself a hotel. . . ."

"I'll turn it over to Mr. Kunkle, let him run it. . . . You do want me to come with you, don't you, Jake?"

Harper looked beyond the girl to the crowd gathered in the street. All were listening intently, enjoying what they were hearing. Only Caleb Lynch, head tipped down, eyes on the ground, seemed unaware of the proceedings.

"You can bet on it," Jake said, smiling. "You get your stuff together while I go buy you a horse. . . . We'll be leaving right away."

Ray Hogan is an author who has inspired a loyal following over the years since he published his first Western novel *Ex-marshal* in 1956. Hogan was born in Willow Springs, Missouri, where his father was town marshal. At five the Hogan family moved to Albuquerque where Ray Hogan still lives in the foothills of the Sandia and Manzano mountains. His father was on the Albuquerque police force and, in later years, owned the Overland Hotel. It was while listening to his father and other old-timers tell tales from the past that Ray was inspired to recast these tales in fiction. From the beginning he did exhaustive research into the history and the people of the Old West and the walls of his study are lined with various firearms, spurs, pictures, books, and memorabilia, about all of which he can talk in dramatic detail. Among his most popular works are the series of books about Shawn Starbuck, a searcher in a quest for a lost brother, who has a clear sense of right and wrong and who is willing to stand up and be counted when it is a question of fairness or justice. His other major series is about lawman John Rye whose reputation has earned him the sobriquet The Doomsday Marshal. 'I've attempted to capture the courage and bravery of those men and women that lived out West and the dangers and problems they had to overcome,' Hogan once remarked. If his lawmen protagonists seem sometimes larger than life, it is because they are men of integrity, heroes who through grit of character and common sense are able to overcome the obstacles they encounter despite often overwhelming odds. This same grit of character can also be found in Hogan's heroines and, in *The Vengeance of Fortuna West*, Hogan wrote a gripping and totally believable account of a woman who takes up the badge and tracks the men who killed her lawman husband by ambush. No less intriguing in her way is Nellie Dupray, convicted of rustling in *The Glory Trail*. Above all, what is most impressive about Hogan's Western novels is the consistent quality with which each is crafted, the compelling depth of his characters, and his ability to juxtapose the complexities of human conflict into narratives always as intensely interesting as they are emotionally involving. His latest novel is *Soldier in Buckskin.*